"You Sure A...
Connor Mu...
Turned To Face Him.

Suddenly all he could think of was kissing her, touching her, peeling that chaste white dress from her ivory skin, then, tasting every last naked inch of her, while she murmured his name into the darkness, again and again and again....

It made no sense. She was covered practically from head to toe, and yet Connor was more turned on than he'd ever been in his life. And he suspected that his arousal had nothing to do with the fact that Winona might be a madam, a mistress of pleasure who knew how to...do things to a man...that would never occur to other women.

No, Connor was afraid his preoccupation with the delicious Winona was the result of something far more insidious than simple lust.

God Almighty, he thought. Could this case possibly get any worse?

Dear Reader,

Welcome to Silhouette Desire! We're delighted to offer you again this month six passionate, powerful and provocative romances sure to please you.

Start with December's fabulous MAN OF THE MONTH, *A Cowboy's Promise*. This latest title in Anne McAllister's popular CODE OF THE WEST miniseries features a rugged Native American determined to win back the woman he left three years before. Then discover *The Secret Life of Connor Monahan* in Elizabeth Bevarly's tale of a vice cop who mistakenly surmises that a prim and proper restaurateur is operating a call-girl ring.

The sizzling miniseries 20 AMBER COURT concludes with Anne Marie Winston's *Risqué Business*, in which a loyal employee tries to prevent a powerful CEO with revenge on his mind from taking over the company she thinks of as her family. Reader favorite Maureen Child delivers the next installment of another exciting miniseries, THE FORTUNES OF TEXAS: THE LOST HEIRS. In *Did You Say Twins?!* a marine sergeant inherits twin daughters and is forced to turn for help to the woman who refused his marriage proposal ten years before.

The sexy hero of *Michael's Temptation,* the last book in Eileen Wilks's TALL, DARK & ELIGIBLE miniseries, goes to Central America to rescue a lovely lady who's been captured by guerrillas. And sparks fly when a smooth charmer and a sassy tomboy are brought together by their shared inheritance of an Australian horse farm in Brownyn Jameson's *Addicted to Nick*.

Take time out from the holiday rush and treat yourself to all six of these not-to-be-missed romances.

Enjoy,

Joan Marlow Golan

Joan Marlow Golan
Senior Editor, Silhouette Desire

Please address questions and book requests to:
Silhouette Reader Service
U.S.: 3010 Walden Ave., P.O. Box 1325, Buffalo, NY 14269
Canadian: P.O. Box 609, Fort Erie, Ont. L2A 5X3

The Secret Life of Connor Monahan

ELIZABETH BEVARLY

Published by Silhouette Books

America's Publisher of Contemporary Romance

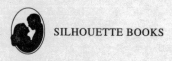

SILHOUETTE BOOKS

ISBN 0-373-76406-5

THE SECRET LIFE OF CONNOR MONAHAN

Copyright © 2001 by Elizabeth Bevarly

This edition published by arrangement with Harlequin Books S.A.

® and TM are trademarks of Harlequin Books S.A., used under license.
Trademarks indicated with ® are registered in the United States Patent
and Trademark Office, the Canadian Trade Marks Office and in other
countries.

Visit Silhouette at www.eHarlequin.com

Printed in U.S.A.

Books by Elizabeth Bevarly

Silhouette Desire

An Unsuitable Man for the Job #724
Jake's Christmas #753
A Lawless Man #856
*A Dad Like Daniel #908
*The Perfect Father #920
*Dr. Daddy #933
†Father of the Brat #993
†Father of the Brood #1005
†Father on the Brink #1016
‡Roxy and the Rich Man #1053
‡Lucy and the Loner #1063
‡Georgia Meets Her Groom #1083
**Bride of the Bad Boy #1124
**Beauty and the Brain #1130
**The Virgin and the Vagabond #1136
The Sheriff and the Impostor Bride #1184
Society Bride #1196
That Boss of Mine #1231
*A Doctor in Her Stocking #1252
*Dr. Mommy #1269
*Dr. Irresistible #1291
First Comes Love #1323
Monahan's Gamble #1337
The Temptation of Rory Monahan #1363
When Jayne Met Erik #1389
The Secret Life of Connor Monahan #1406

Silhouette Special Edition

Destinations South #557
Close Range #590
Donovan's Chance #639
Moriah's Mutiny #676
Up Close #737
Hired Hand #803
Return Engagement #844

*From Here to Maternity
†From Here to Paternity
‡The Family McCormick
**Blame It on Bob

ELIZABETH BEVARLY

was born and raised in Louisville, Kentucky, and earned her B.A. with honors in English from the University of Louisville in 1983. When she's not writing, the RITA-nominated author enjoys old movies, old houses, good books, whimsical antiques, hot jazz and even hotter salsa (the music, not the sauce). She resides with her husband and young son back home in Kentucky.

For Dad

One

Winona Thornbury was up to her elbows in trouble, and, ever the optimist, was trying to assure herself that things couldn't possibly get any worse, when, naturally, things got worse. Really worse.

The up-to-her-elbows-in-trouble part came in the form of a large chocolate bombe she had fashioned for the evening's dessert at her self-named restaurant, Winona's. She was putting the finishing touches on said bombe—a delicate ring of ripe, red raspberries—when one of her waiters came scurrying into the kitchen much too fast, and careened right into her back. And before she could say *"Pardonnez moi"*—not that *she* had done anything for which she needed to say *pardonnez*—Winona was biceps-deep in chocolate bombe, something that did nothing to enhance the once-white chef's jacket that had been so crisp and clean when she had donned it earlier that afternoon.

Wonderful, she thought as she extracted her arm from the icy confection. Now what was she supposed to serve for dessert tonight? Although her restaurant was famous for its delicious and innovative sweets, Winona was reasonably certain that chocolate-bombe-with-arm-hole wasn't going to go over well with her patrons, even with the ring of ripe, red raspberries. It would probably be even less popular with the Bloomington, Indiana, health department. Fortunately, she had experimented with cheesecakes earlier that afternoon, some of which had turned out surprisingly well. They would just have to do.

However, no sooner had she settled that problem than did the things-got-worse-really-worse part arrive. It came in the form of a request from the hostess stand, a request her waiter had been about to relay before he stumbled into her. The message itself went something like, "Oh, my God, Winona, come out here quick. Hurry, hurry, we're in big, big trouble." Doing her best to wipe what she could of the chocolate bombe from her sleeve—which, unfortunately, wasn't much—Winona went rushing from the kitchen forthwith.

It was seven o'clock on a Friday night—a lovely September evening with just a hint of autumn in the air—and Winona's was packed, now that classes were back in session at the nearby Indiana University. Even the bar was full—either with people who were stopping in for a cocktail on their way home from work or class, or with people who were waiting for a table to open up so that they could dine.

The restaurant's regular patrons were an eclectic assortment of pin-striped local businesspeople and casually dressed teachers and students—mostly graduate and postgraduate. History and English majors in particular seemed to favor Winona's. But that was probably because of the decor as much as it was because of the menu and extensive wine list. Being something of a romantic person—actually, being a fanatically romantic person—Winona Thornbury tended to live quite shamelessly in the past, and everything about her reflected that. As a result, her restaurant was a very accurate reflection of turn-of-the-century America.

She had purchased the big Victorian house three years ago with her half of a modest inheritance that she and her sister, Miriam, had received from an elderly aunt. Winona, being thrifty and talented as well as romantic, had then completed the bulk of the renovation work and decoration herself while working full-time as a pastry chef at another local restaurant. She'd spared no expense—or elbow grease—in turning the dilapidated building into a show-place, comparable to any Tuxedo Park estate circa 1900ish.

In fact, the restaurant's decor very much resembled a turn-of-the-century luxury hotel, quite elegant, quite opulent, quite abundant. Lace curtains and silk moiré draperies framed the floor-to-ceiling windows in every room, and more lace and moiré covered each of the tables. The color schemes varied from room to room, but Winona had opted mostly for dark jewel tones and contrasting color schemes throughout. The main dining room was ruby and emerald, the smaller salon dining room was sapphire and topaz, while the patio dining room was amethyst and coral.

Her slogan for the restaurant was "At Winona's everybody feels at home." And, indeed, anyone who dined there would agree with the statement wholeheartedly. Less than a year after opening, Winona's was *the* place to dine in Hoosierland—because there was nothing in Winona's that wasn't finely crafted and genuinely beautiful, not to mention extremely tasteful. Including the food. Especially the food. That, primarily was what brought her patrons back again and again.

Well, that, and the telephones.

Because somewhere along the line, before opening her establishment, Winona had come up with the idea of putting an antique telephone at the center of each table, all of them wired together within the restaurant, so that patrons could telephone each other from one table to the next. Elaborately calligraphied numbers hung above the antique lamps that hovered over each table, and by dialing that number from one's own table, one could contact whomever was seated elsewhere.

So far, the telephones had proved to be great fun and good conversation starters. There had even been one or two romantic entanglements that had resulted from the gimmick. In fact, one couple was renting out Winona's this month for their wedding reception, specifically because they had met while flirting over the telephones on opening night. Winona had been delighted when the couple had called to make the arrangements, and had found the whole idea to be enchanting.

Tonight, however, she wasn't delighted *or* enchanted. Because tonight, for the first time since she had opened the restaurant, *nothing* was going right.

Her head chef had called in that afternoon with something highly unpleasant and even more highly contagious, and Winona hadn't been able to find anyone who could come in to cover for him. As a result, she was trying to complete the work of *two* chefs tonight, in addition to her owner/manager duties. Ruthie, her expediter, was working with a bad ankle, thanks to a hiking accident the day before, making her anything *but* expedient. And Winona had discovered earlier that morning that the alleged organic farmer from whom she had been purchasing alleged organic produce—and specifying, *not* alleging, on the menu as such—was, in fact, using chemicals on his decidedly unorganic harvests.

And as if all that weren't enough, when Winona left the kitchen to go to the hostess stand and uncover whatever *else* was about to go wrong, she discovered the most troubling thing of all.

He was here again.

And as troubling as his appearance was, a little thrill of excitement shimmied right up her spine to see *him* sitting there, gazing at her in his usual way—as if he wanted to make *her* his dessert tonight.

Actually, if she were honest with herself—and truly, Winona did always try to be honest with herself—she would be forced to admit that, normally, his arrival wouldn't necessarily be something she considered to be going wrong. Because, normally, she liked seeing *him* in the restaurant, even if his...attentions...were just a *tad* forward.

Then again, normally, when *he* came to the restaurant, Winona wasn't frazzled and high-strung and overwrought, not to mention bedecked in once-white chef's togs that were now splattered with 99 percent of the evening's recommended selections—never mind the chocolate sleeve. The last thing she needed or wanted was for *him* to see her like this. Even if she had no idea who *he* really was.

She did know, however, that he was exceedingly attractive. His jet-black hair and ice-blue eyes made for a combination Winona had never been able to resist, and his features were almost blindingly handsome. He easily topped six feet, his broad shoulders and back straining against the seams of his expertly, and expensively, tailored dark suits. His silk neckties, clearly expensive, and his understated—but likewise expensive—wristwatch suggested he came from a moneyed background, and he fairly oozed wealth and success and refinement.

Winona suspected he was a newly transferred executive who had come to work in a regional corporate office of some kind. Perhaps he even lived as far away as Indianapolis. She was fairly certain, at least, that he wasn't a native of Bloomington. He just didn't seem to have that local air about him. But for the past few weeks, he had been coming in for dinner once or twice a week. He always arrived alone. And he always dined alone. And he always left alone. And he always seemed to be watching Winona *very* intently.

It was just too bad that he was so young, she invariably

thought when she saw him. Not that she had a problem with such age differences—not for other people at any rate. She herself, however, already suffered from a significant generational disadvantage—namely that she had been born about four generations too late. It was something that made her soul, at least, more than a hundred years old.

The mysterious stranger, on the other hand, must be at least ten years younger than her own thirty-eight, temporally and chronologically speaking at any rate, because he couldn't possibly have yet hit thirty himself. And in addition to his young age, he was clearly upscale, trendy, hip…and thoroughly modern. He was all those things that Winona herself most certainly was not. Which made all the more puzzling his interest in her. Because clearly, he *was* interested in her. Because, clearly, he *did* watch her very intently whenever he dined at her restaurant.

Just as he was doing tonight.

Winona did her best to avoid his attention as she skirted the edge of the main dining room, hoping to keep a low profile—she didn't want *any* of her patrons to see her bedecked in chef's-previously-whites-with-a-chocolate-sleeve. She had won herself a reputation for being tidy and well organized, in addition to her proudly worn mantle of nice, old-fashioned girl, and she never appeared in her restaurant in, shall we say, dishabille. No, whenever Winona made an appearance in the dining room, she always made sure she looked as if she had just been cast as an extra on the set of the movie *Titanic*.

Tonight, however, she much more resembled a chip of the iceberg. A very messy chip at that.

"What's the problem?" she asked Laurel, her hostess—who, like the rest of the staff, *was* dressed as if she'd just been cast as an extra for the movie *Titanic*—when she arrived at the hostess stand.

"It's the Carlton party," Laurel said.

"What about the Carlton party?" Winona asked. "They're not coming until tomorrow night."

Laurel shook her head. "No, they're here tonight."

Winona gazed blankly at her hostess, certain she'd misheard. "But they're not supposed to be here until *tomorrow* night," she said again. "They made a reservation for *tomorrow* night. Saturday night."

Winona knew they had, because she'd taken the reservation herself a month ago and reconfirmed it just the week before. Granted, she may have uttered the date of the reservation when doing so, as opposed to the day of the week, but that was beside the point. Either Edna Carlton's calendar was wrong, or Winona's was. And with all due respect to Mrs. Carlton, Winona was certain she herself had, as always, recorded the correct date and time. She simply did not make mistakes like that.

"That's not what they're saying," Laurel told her. "Mrs. Carlton insists the reservation was for tonight. And she's brought the entire party. And they want to be seated. Now."

"All *twelve* of them?" Winona asked incredulously. "They want to be seated *now?*"

"Actually, there are fourteen of them," Laurel told her. "Mrs. Carlton decided at the last minute to invite another couple, because she was sure you'd be able to accommodate them. And yes," the hostess added, "they want to be seated *now.*"

Winona eyed the other woman with much panic. "Oh. No."

Laurel nodded. "That was pretty much my reaction, too."

Winona thought fast. "All right. We can handle this. We can. We'll just…"

Run away, was her initial reaction. But she quickly saw the inappropriateness of that. "We'll just…" she began again. "Just…just…" And then she brightened. "We'll seat them upstairs, in my dining room."

"*Your* dining room?" Laurel echoed with disbelief. "But you *live* upstairs. Those are your *private* quarters."

"Not anymore, they're not," Winona told her. "Now they're our special party room. Find Teddy and Max and tell them to run upstairs and set the table for fourteen." Thank goodness her table sat that many, Winona couldn't help thinking. And that was the maximum limit. "And tell them to use my china, crystal and silver that's in the bottom of the china cabinet," she continued hastily. "They'll have to mix and match, but it will be faster that way—they won't have to lug anything up the stairs. Then tell Teddy to give his tables down here to Max and Stephanie, and take the Carlton party himself."

She thought for a few minutes more, to see if there were any problems with the plan. And although there were indeed one or two—or fourteen—they were nothing she couldn't handle. Probably.

"Yes," she finally said with a decisive nod, "that should work out just fine."

Except that the service wasn't likely to be up to snuff, Winona thought. Not for the Carlton party, and not for the main dining room, either. And having such a large party was bound to slow up the food preparation for the other diners. Then again, if she opened a couple of cases of champagne and had the servers present each of their tables with complimentary glasses…

Maybe, just maybe, all would be well.

Winona spun back around to return to the kitchen, only to find herself staring at *him* again. And, drat it all, he was staring back at her. Very intently, too. Worse than that, he was running the pad of his middle finger slowly around the rim of his wineglass, and somehow making the leisurely journey seem inexplicably—and profoundly—erotic.

For one brief, electric moment, their gazes held firm, and

Winona felt a shiver of something inexplicable and unwarranted—and very, *very* warm—go shimmying right down her spine. Her reaction made no sense. She had no idea who or what the man was, or why he kept coming into her restaurant.

But there was something in his eyes in that scintillating moment, something fierce and knowing and determined and…and…and—*oh, my*—and *hot,* that told her it wouldn't be long before she found out.

Battling a sudden fever that seemed to come out of nowhere, Winona fled to the kitchen and tried to forget about the handsome, young, mysterious—hot—stranger. Somehow, though, she knew he wasn't likely to stray far from her thoughts.

Detective Connor Monahan fastened his gaze to the fleeing backside of Winona Thornbury as he lifted his glass by the stem to sip carefully—and only the smallest amount—from the ruby liquid inside. But his reaction wasn't due to the fact that her backside was an especially pleasant thing to gaze upon, though indeed it was quite pleasant. No, the real reason Connor watched his quarry with such interest was that he was wondering how much longer it would be before he finally nailed the woman for her numerous and colorful crimes.

He'd worked some interesting cases since being bumped up to the Vice Squad nearly a year ago, but never one like this. Never such an elaborately organized and stealthily operated prostitution ring, and never one that worked out of an allegedly respectable establishment like this one, with an allegedly respectable proprietress like Winona Thornbury. Because in spite of her alleged respectability, Winona Thornbury was, in a word, very luscious.

Okay, so that was two words. Sue him. One word just didn't seem like enough for a woman like her.

Though, granted, tonight she didn't seem to be quite up

to her usual very luscious standards. Where before she'd always been dressed in some kind of turn-of-the-century getup that made her look like a nice, old-fashioned girl—yeah, right—tonight she looked more like a chef-in-training. A chef-in-training who wasn't training particularly well, at that. Not unless one chocolate sleeve and a long, bedraggled braid was all the rage for chefs in the know.

Usually, though, she really did look like a nice, old-fashioned girl—*as if*—with her pale gold hair all piled atop her head, and wearing antique-looking dresses that she might have found in her great-great-great-grandmother's hope chest. Or else she wore a white embroidered blouse with a high collar and a million buttons up the back, coupled with some long skirt that swished around button-booted ankles.

But no matter how much she buttoned herself up and battened herself down, no matter how nice and old-fashioned her clothes were, Winona Thornbury couldn't hide her lusciousness. Because even whalebone couldn't restrain the curves that woman possessed.

But then, of course she was luscious, Connor reminded himself. She was a high-class madam who ran one of the most exclusive—and elusive—call-girl rings in Indiana. As such, she'd almost certainly started off her career as a call girl herself. And only the most luscious call girls made enough money to go into business for themselves.

And what a business. Oh, sure. Winona's might look like a legitimate four-star restaurant on the outside, but the interior fairly shrieked *brothel*. Hell, the furnishings alone had probably started off life in some house of ill repute. What person in their right mind would furnish a place like this, if not because they wanted to evoke a certain, oh…mood? And what woman dressed like that, if not to hide what she really was?

And why would a restaurant have telephones on the table, for criminy's sake, he thought further, if not to make illicit assignations? Sure, it might look like a cute gimmick, but Connor Monahan—along with the Bloomington PD and the Indiana State Police—knew better.

There was all kinds of evidence to indicate that a ring of call girls was working out of Winona's. All Connor and his colleagues had to do now was find the person in charge. Or, at least, uncover solid evidence against the person in charge. Because Connor, for one, knew it was Winona Thornbury masterminding the operation, even if some of his colleagues had their doubts. Even if some of his colleagues were convinced that, although there was most certainly a call-girl ring operating out of the place, Winona Thornbury herself was oblivious to the fact.

Hell, those guys were just smitten, that was all, Connor thought. They'd just fallen for the nice, old-fashioned girl—oh, sure—routine. Not that he could much blame them. If he wasn't such a pragmatic guy—not to mention if he wasn't totally mistrustful of women in general, and luscious women in particular, though not without good reason, dammit—he'd be smitten, too. But he knew better. He knew Winona Thornbury was guilty of pandering, and he intended to prove it. Once he had that solid evidence in hand, then they could bust some lamb chops.

By now Winona Thornbury had disappeared into the kitchen, so Connor glanced down at the menu that lay open on the table before him. Hmm, he thought as he perused the selections. The lamb chops *did* look rather nice this evening....

But then, everything in Winona's looked nice. Especially Madam Winona herself.

Oh, it was going to be such a pleasure to bring that woman down, he thought. And he tried not to think about how *bringing down* Winona Thornbury suddenly took on an entirely different connotation than the one vice cops traditionally entertained.

Pushing the thought aside, he gazed at the telephone on

his table and silently willed it to ring. *Ring, dammit,* he commanded. Why didn't it ever ring for him? He and the boys on the Bloomington PD had been staking out Winona's for three weeks now, and they had yet to get a nibble, even though they knew—they *knew*—there was a ring of call girls working out of the place. Connor had been chosen among the men to be the bait, because he'd seemed the most likely to carry off the charade of successful businessman. And also because, he'd assured the others, there wasn't a woman on the planet who could resist him.

Okay, so maybe he'd been lying about that last part. *Most* women couldn't resist him. Well, several, anyway. He could think of at least three, right off the top of his head. So why wasn't his telephone ringing? he wondered. Why hadn't it rung any of the half-dozen times he'd come into the restaurant over the last few weeks? Why did it always just sit there, mocking him?

He couldn't blame it on faulty wiring, because he'd sat at different tables on nearly every occasion. And as he gazed around the room now, he saw a number of patrons chatting amiably on their phones, some of them seated at tables he'd occupied himself on previous evenings. So why wasn't anyone calling *him?*

As if jarred by his mental meanderings, the telephone on his table did suddenly ring, jarring him from his mental meanderings. Immediately Connor snatched up the receiver and placed it by his ear. Leaning forward, he forced his voice to remain steady and calm as he spoke into the mouthpiece. "Hello?"

There was a slight pause from the other end, then a man's voice said, "Oh. I'm sorry. I seem to have the wrong number. I was trying to reach the redhead at table fifteen."

"No problem," Connor muttered irritably into the mouthpiece. All for nothing. Because the man had already hung up.

He turned his attention to table fifteen then, which was

immediately to the left of his own. Sure enough, a rather breathtaking redhead was seated there—alone.

Hmmm, Connor thought.

As he watched, her telephone rang, no doubt due to the gent who had just erroneously called Connor. The redhead answered the telephone with a low, throaty greeting, then smiled and began to murmur something he couldn't hear into the phone.

Connor sighed. Damn. That was probably one of the very illicit assignations he was supposed to be halting being arranged right there under his nose. Because the redhead certainly had the look of a high-priced call girl. Meaning that she was dressed in an elegant, and very modest, black cocktail dress, with understated jewelry and makeup and simply arranged hair.

That was the problem with call girls these days, he thought. They all looked like debutantes and corporate interns. She was probably a student from the university. An economics major, he couldn't help thinking further, making a few extra bucks on the side.

Man. What was the youth of today coming to?

Within moments of hanging up her telephone, the redhead was joined at her table by a man old enough to be her father. Connor watched to see if maybe she'd slip up and do something incriminating—like loudly demand cash up-front for very specific sexual services she would render right there at the table for all to see—only to have her and her companion open their menus and peruse the evening's selections.

Well, of course, he thought. What woman was going to give it up without getting a steak dinner out of it first, even if she would be paid handsomely for her efforts at evening's end?

Connor sighed his frustration and willed the telephone on his table to ring again. But it never did. Not even after he'd ordered dinner, and not even after he'd finished eating the dinner he ordered.

The only thing that kept him from sinking into a totally black humor was the fact that, eventually, Winona Thornbury appeared in the dining room again. She was still dressed as a chef, but had changed into a clean jacket. And she must have taken the time to rebraid her hair, he noted, because the length of gold that fell to her waist now was much tidier than it had been before.

All in all, Connor thought, she really did appear to be harmless. Of course, he'd had the same thoughts about other women of his acquaintance—one in particular—and look how that had turned out.

Maybe it was time for him to stop waiting around for something to happen with this case and take matters into his own hands, he thought. Not that he wanted to skirt the edge of entrapment or anything, but maybe a nudge in the right direction would get things rolling.

Like maybe, he thought as he watched Winona Thornbury make her way to the hostess stand, it was time he paid his compliments—among other things—to the chef.

TWO

By midnight Winona was ready to collapse—such had been the evening's toll on her. Only one more hour, she told herself as she carried the bar and restaurant receipts and cash register drawers up the stairs to her office. You can last one more hour. On weekends the kitchen closed at precisely eleven o'clock, the bar followed at precisely twelve, and, usually, all of her employees were gone by precisely 1:00 a.m. Laurel, or whichever of her other hostesses or hosts was working on any given night, would take care of winding things up downstairs while Winona did the numbers work upstairs. It was a system that generally worked very well.

Tonight, however, all Winona wanted to do was escape into sleep. To nestle herself down into the feather bed that lay atop her regular mattress, and snuggle under the cool, lavender-scented cotton sheets, and lose herself in sweet slumber until dawn crept over the windowsill tomorrow. Instead she groaned with much feeling when she passed by her miniscule kitchen on the way to her office and beheld the mess that awaited her there.

She had told Teddy to simply clear away the dishes from the Carlton party as he would any other group of diners and leave them in her kitchen, and then to return to work downstairs the moment the party left. She hadn't wanted to disrupt the flow of the restaurant's pace any more than she had already by robbing it of one of its servers, and at the time Winona hadn't minded performing the cleanup herself. Now, however...

She sighed heavily. Now the last thing she felt like doing was hand washing and drying all the fine crystal, china and silver left over from fourteen people. But she couldn't very well put her antique serveware in the restaurant's hobart, could she? The delicate pieces would fairly dissolve under the strength of the water pressure and detergent. And she wasn't about to ask Teddy or any of the others to wash them after the exhausting night they'd all just survived.

No, this was Winona's responsibility, and one which she would dispose of forthwith. Because there was no way she could go to bed knowing what clutter and squalor remained in her kitchen. The very thought of sleeping with all that in there sent a shudder of distaste winding through her entire body.

With another heartfelt sigh she went to her office to lock up the night's receipts—she could do her numbers work tomorrow morning. Then she went to her bedroom to shed her stained and bedraggled chef's togs and slipped on an ankle-length, sleeveless, embroidered white cotton nightgown in its place. To protect her sleepwear from the mess she was about to assail, she tugged a long, flowered cotton robe over it, then tucked her feet into a pair of tapestry slippers. Then she wound her braid around the top of her head a couple of times, headband fashion, and pinned it in back, to keep it out of her way.

There. That was better. No one would be seeing her for

the rest of the night, after all, so she could, as they said in the old movies, slip into something a little more comfortable. Except for Laurel, of course, who would come up later to tell Winona that all was well and that she would be locking up on her way out. Winona herself always performed a final check of the premises before turning in, but for now, she could relax.

Relax and wash dishes leftover from fourteen people.

She sighed yet again. Ah, well. There was nothing else for it. She made her way to the kitchen, shoved up the sleeves of her robe and went to work. She had finished scraping and had just submerged the first stack of plates into the soapy water of her old-fashioned porcelain double sink when she heard a soft whuffle of sound coming from nearby and turned toward it.

And then she gasped when she saw *him* standing framed by her kitchen doorway, one forearm braced on each side, his entire body leaning forward. His dark hair fell recklessly over his forehead, and his ice-blue eyes were fixed on hers, blazing with much...with much...much...

Oh, *my.*

Winona swallowed with some difficulty as an eddy of heat purled through her midsection, but somehow she remembered to breathe. For the life of her, though, she couldn't move a muscle, couldn't so much as bat an eye, so enthralled was she by his mere appearance.

He was still wearing his dark, elegant suit, but he, too, had clearly made himself more comfortable some time ago. Now the jacket hung open casually, and the silk necktie dangled unfettered from his collar. The top two buttons of his white dress shirt were unfastened, revealing a strong column of tanned throat, and a hint of the dark hair that must be scattered richly across his chest.

Winona felt herself blush at witnessing such a thing, harmless though the vision might seem to most people. After all, men revealed more than *he* was revealing now at the beach or swimming pool, didn't they? Then again, she had always avoided swimming pools and beaches for that very reason—she simply was not comfortable being around people who were only half, or less, clothed. And now, to see *him* in such a state…

Well. It simply ignited her imagination in ways she would just as soon not have it be ignited. Because suddenly, her imagination was filled with visions of *him*. Worse, it was filled with visions of *him* and…*her*. And they were doing things no one in Winona's imagination had *ever* done before.

Not that she was a complete innocent—oh, no. By some standards she was a vastly experienced woman. Like, for example, by a four-year-old's standards. But Winona did know what went on between a man and a woman. Fairly well, actually, in spite of never allowing the lights on when that man-woman thing went on. She had been engaged once, after all. She wasn't a virgin. Not quite.

But that was all beside the point now. The point now was that *he* was standing in her private quarters, in a state of dishabille. Worse than that, *she* was standing in her private quarters with him, in an even greater state of dishabille. And Winona had no idea how to react to such a development. It had been years since she'd been in a state of dishabille with a man. And she'd certainly never done so with a man whose name she didn't even know.

Thinking for a moment that she must only be imagining *him* here, she closed her eyes briefly and counted to three, as if doing so might magically dispel the vision. But when she opened her eyes again, there he still stood, gazing at her in that maddening way he had of gazing at her—as if he wanted to consume her in one big, voracious bite.

"Hi," he said. And not at all voraciously, Winona couldn't help remarking. No, his was a simple how-do-you-do sort of greeting, totally lacking in intent. Realizing that, however, did nothing to ease her concern.

She blinked her confusion and replied automatically, "Hello." Then, kicking herself into gear again, she added, "Can I help you?" The question felt a bit odd, all things considered, because the last thing Winona wanted to do was help a total stranger with questionable intentions who had invaded the privacy of her home. But she was, above all things, courteous, and she didn't wish to come across as a harridan on their first meeting, even if that first meeting consisted of him having invaded the privacy of her home.

Not that she wanted to imply, to herself or anyone, that there would be a *second* meeting, she quickly qualified to herself—especially if that meeting, too, involved violating her privacy. In any case, implying such a thing would be much too forward. Still, she did want to be polite.

Plus, she knew that if she screamed at the top of her lungs right now, however frightfully discourteous that might seem, someone downstairs was bound to hear her and come rushing to her aid. Probably. So there was that.

And she was considering doing just that, in spite of its discourtesy—and she was also considering whether or not she should hurl herself out the window and onto the fire escape, again at the risk of seeming impolite—when the man smiled.

And oh, *my,* if she had thought him handsome before, when he smiled the way he did then, he was…he was…he was…

Oh, *my.*

"I was, um… I was just looking for the men's room," he said with a self-conscious shrug. "I spilled something on my jacket," he hastened to qualify, pointing to a small stain just above his left pocket. "Guess I took a wrong turn, huh?"

She nodded slowly, still too entranced by his smile and the way it seemed to soften his otherwise rugged features, to have her full wits about her. "The facilities are downstairs," she told him. "In the restaurant. I'm afraid this is a private residence."

His mouth—that generous, beautiful mouth—dropped open a bit, and he emitted a single, nervous chuckle. "Oh, man, I really am sorry. I saw a big party of people come down the stairs earlier, and I just assumed there was more of the restaurant up here. When I couldn't find the... facilities—" he smiled a bit indulgently at the word, almost as if he were mocking her, Winona couldn't help thinking "—downstairs, I assumed they were up here."

She smiled, albeit a bit anxiously. His explanation made perfect sense and offered a reasonable excuse for his appearance. Why, then, was she having so much trouble believing him? Why did she feel as though he was acting out some kind of charade? Why did she get the impression that he wasn't being honest with her? Because for some reason, she didn't think he was being honest with her. She had no idea why.

"Well, there *was* a large party of diners up here this evening," she conceded. "But that was due to special circumstances. Normally this part of Winona's is off-limits to patrons."

She was about to conclude with a very meaningful, very adamant—but very polite—*Good-night, sir,* but was halted by his expression. It had changed dramatically the moment she'd uttered the words, *special circumstances.*

Then, "Special circumstances?" he repeated avidly. He punctuated the question by arching his dark eyebrows, and his blue eyes fairly twinkled with his—rather extreme—interest. She had no idea why he should be showing such an inordinate amount of attention to the Carlton party, and she had no idea how she should reply.

So she only nodded warily and told him, "Yes. Special circumstances."

"What, uh...what kind of special circumstances?" he asked, still seeming far too interested in such a simple thing. And he actually seemed to be awaiting her reply with his breath held.

"It was a large party for whom I was unprepared," she told him. "The facilities downstairs wouldn't have adequately accommodated their needs."

But even that didn't seem to satisfy the man's curiosity, because he grew even more avid. "Unprepared?" he echoed. "Wouldn't have accommodated their needs?" He tipped his head forward, now clearly very interested. "In what way? Just what kind of *needs* did they have?"

What on earth was going on? Winona wondered. Why was this man so fascinated by the Carltons? Were they in some kind of trouble? But that was ridiculous. The Carltons were one of Bloomington's oldest, finest and most upstanding families.

"In the way that I didn't have room for them," Winona told him cautiously.

"Well, just what kind of room did you need?" he asked.

She narrowed her eyes at him, with much of her own interest now. Just what was he up to? "Not that it's any of your business, Mr...."

"Montgomery," he replied without compunction. His smile suddenly dazzling. "Connor Montgomery."

She dipped her chin deftly in acknowledgment. "Not that it's any of your business, Mr. Montgomery," she began again, "but there was some confusion with a reservation, and, unexpectedly, I found myself with need for a table to accommodate fourteen people, at seven o'clock sharp. I didn't have that downstairs, so I seated the party up here instead. It was the best I could manage on short notice."

He gazed at her intently for a moment, as if he were taking great care to process that information. Then, finally, "Oh," he said. "I see." His entire body seemed to relax, and only then did she realize how tense he had been during his interrogation.

How very curious, she thought. Who on earth was he,

and what was he doing here? And why did she feel so suspicious of his motives? Toward the Carltons…and toward her, too.

"Connor," she said thoughtfully, wondering why she was even bothering to prolong their conversation. Perhaps she simply wanted to assuage her curiosity about him. Or perhaps she was hoping to uncover some explanation for his real reason for coming upstairs, should the one he voiced actually be some kind of deception, as she suspected it was.

Or perhaps, she thought further, it was for some other reason entirely, one she shouldn't be thinking about, let alone acting upon. Nevertheless, "That's a nice, old-fashioned name, isn't it?" she asked him.

He shrugged…and didn't seem to be especially interested in putting an end to their dialogue yet, either. Because he leaned one shoulder against the doorway now, crossing one leg over the other in a casual stance that seemed, somehow, in no way casual. "Maybe," he replied. He smiled devilishly—for truly, there was no other way to describe his expression then but naughty. "But I'm *not* a nice, old-fashioned guy."

Well, that was more than obvious, Winona thought as another thrill of heat rushed through her midsection, pooling in a place she would just as soon not be feeling heat right now—not in mixed company, at any rate. "Well," she tried instead, suddenly thinking that it might not be such a good idea to prolong this conversation after all, "as I said, the facilities are downstairs, so if you'll—"

"Mind if I just use your sink?" he asked impulsively, moving forward toward the washbasin in question. "I'm here, it's convenient, what the hell, right?"

Winona opened her mouth to object, but before she had the chance, he was shrugging out of his jacket, and his shirt was gaping open at the collar, and she was gazing at that dark hair again, and her imagination was igniting once more—oh, my goodness, was it igniting once more—and all she could do was stare as he approached.

Stare and take a step backward for each one that he took forward, gaping in amazement that he would be so bold and that she would be so passive. Just because she was a nice, old-fashioned girl didn't mean Winona Thornbury was a pushover. The one thing she did like about the twentieth century—and its ensuing new millennium—was that it had brought enormous freedom to her gender. So she had no trouble whatsoever putting her slippered little foot down, when times called for such a drastic measure. Usually. For some reason, though, with Connor Montgomery, all Winona wanted to do was retreat, as quickly as her slippered little feet would allow.

"It's probably just a little Jameson," he told her, as he stopped at the sink, seeming oblivious to her more-than-obvious retreat—she was, after all, fairly cowering in the corner by now. "It'll probably come right out," he added. He swiveled the spigot to the other side of the sink, then turned on the hot water and thrust his long, middle finger under the flow of water to test its temperature. "I'll just be a minute."

For some reason, as Winona watched the warm water rush over his finger, as she noted the way the stream parted so readily over that strong digit, as she remarked the way he crooked his knuckle and turned it first one way then the other, as she watched his finger curl and flex and curl again…

Well. For some reason she couldn't utter a sound. For some reason she couldn't move a muscle. For some reason all she could do was stand there and stare like an idiot, marveling at the dark, frantic ribbon of wanting that wound slowly, hotly, through her. Because behind that ribbon of wanting trailed a desire so keen, so querulous, it was unlike anything she had ever felt before. And Winona was utterly unprepared for it.

"Too hot," she whispered as she continued to gaze at the finger that cleaved the hot water with such finesse. Without even realizing she was doing it, she lifted a hand to her neck, curling her fingers loosely about her throat as she murmured further, "Much, *much* too hot."

Amazingly, Connor Montgomery heard her over the rush, because he glanced up to look at her as she uttered the brief, nearly incoherent, statement. His expression as he withdrew his hand from beneath the spigot, however, indicated that his mind was not on the temperature of the water, but instead was focused more on the temperature of…Winona? And strangely, her temperature did seem to be a bit…off.

For one long moment, they only stared at each other in a dazed sort of silence, neither seeming to comprehend the sudden sizzle of frantic heat that arced between them. Then Connor's gaze darted from Winona's eyes to her hair, then to her jaw, then to her mouth. Then lower, to the hand she had circled defensively around her throat, then to the bare wrist and arm above, then lower again, to her breasts, to her hips, to her legs and to her breasts again. Then back to her face, to her mouth, where his gaze lingered for a long time. His cheeks were growing ruddy now, presumably from the heat of the steam rising from the still-rushing water. Or, perhaps, that was the result of something else entirely.

"The water," Winona finally managed to clarify, the words coming out weakly for some reason. In fact, her entire body felt weak for some reason. "You're running the…the water…too hot. Cold water will work better for a stain on that fabric."

But he seemed not to hear her—albeit quiet—words, because his attention was still focused wholly on her mouth. His own lips were slightly parted, as if he were having a little trouble breathing, but his chest rose and fell a bit rapidly, so surely he was indeed getting enough air.

And then, without warning, without speaking, he turned off the water. Then, likewise without warning, without speaking, he took a small step toward Winona. Then another. And another. And another.

The soft scuffing of his shoes over the tile floor echoed wildly through her brain, making the silence surrounding them seem to come alive somehow. Winona told herself she should be frightened of him, reminded herself that she was up here alone with a man she didn't know, one who had been behaving rather oddly. He towered over her scant five foot two by a good foot, outweighed her by a good sixty or seventy pounds. He could easily overpower her. Could easily have his way with her. Could easily—

She told herself to scream, to run away. But her instincts, which had always been very good, assured her that she had nothing to fear. And she wasn't afraid of him, she was surprised to discover. She had no idea why. Somehow, though, he didn't seem at all dangerous. Not in the way she thought he should seem dangerous, at any rate. So she only watched him as he drew nearer. Nearer. And nearer still. Only when there was scarcely a breath of air separating them did Connor Montgomery come to a halt. But he said not one word to explain his actions. He only continued to gaze silently down at her face, studying her mouth as if he had some serious plans for it.

But that was all right, at least for the moment, Winona decided. She had to tip her head back to do it, but his nearness offered her a chance to study him in return. Only it was his eyes that fascinated her so, the way the clear-blue depths seemed to go on forever, starting off at the edges the color of a summer sky, darkening gradually to sapphire, then becoming darker still at the pupils, until the black and midnight hues merged into one. His sable lashes were long and thick, yet somehow they were in no way feminine. No, this man was masculine through and through.

His features, though elegant and refined, were sharp and virile. His build was lean and muscular.

Potent, she thought. That was what he was. Potent and narcotic and more man than Winona was accustomed to encountering.

She swallowed hard at the realization, and his gaze dipped instantly to her throat, his lips parting once again. She wondered if he could see her pulse beating erratically there, so quickly was her blood racing through her body by now. And then his eyes were fixed on hers once more, and Winona found it difficult to breathe. She felt his heat surround her, envelop her, calling to something wild and primitive inside her, something that wanted to answer him with an equally feral, uncivilized response. There was no way she could explain her odd reaction to him. But it was there all the same.

Somehow, though, she resisted his pull. She had never been one for spontaneity, nor was it her custom to succumb so readily to a complete stranger. Heavens, she didn't even succumb to men she knew well. And she certainly wasn't going to allow this bizarre episode to be her introduction to such an impromptu. Regardless of Connor Montgomery's peculiar, almost unearthly command over her, she reined in her inexplicable need to respond.

Until he repeated, "Too hot?" in the sweetest, most sensual voice she had ever heard.

And then she felt the rush of heat winding through her again, urging her to follow her desire instead of her reason.

She had to force herself to remain rooted to the spot. She nodded feebly as she softly replied, "Yes. Too hot." Then, in a final attempt to hang on to reality, she added, "The water, I mean. You had it running too hot."

His mouth crooked up at one corner. "Just the water?" he asked smoothly, his voice feeling like an erotic caress over her hot skin. "Or did I have something else…some*one* else…running too hot, too?"

This time she shook her head slowly, but somehow she couldn't quite pull her gaze from his. "I don't know what you mean, Mr. Montgomery."

He dipped his head just an infinitesimal notch closer to hers. "Don't you?"

She shook her head again, with a bit more fortitude this time. "No. I don't." She straightened some as she pulled back from him, telling herself not to be cowed by this man. And she stated more vigorously now, "As I said, the facilities are downstairs. I'll thank you to use those, instead of me. I mean, instead of mine."

But her correction came too late, as he had clearly heard her slip. Worse, he clearly understood it for the Freudian one it was.

"I see," he said softly, his mouth crooking up at the other corner now. But he didn't move away.

"Mr. Montgomery, please," Winona said, her voice breaking just the slightest bit on that last word.

And only then did the spell finally break, as if she had uttered a charmed incantation to drive the magic away. With one final perusal of her face, her mouth, Connor Montgomery stepped away, taking his heat, his influence, with him. And when he did, Winona felt as cold and alone as she had ever felt in her life. Her reaction was curious, to say the least, for her house was actually warmer than usual, and she was wearing two layers of clothing. But somehow, Connor Montgomery's withdrawal brought an uncomfortable chill behind it.

And that chill grew colder still as he moved completely away, turning to collect his jacket from the counter where he had tossed it some moments ago.

Moments, Winona marveled. Only moments had passed since she'd glanced up from her work to see *him* standing at her door. Yet somehow she felt as if decades had passed instead. As if she'd lived an entire life of love and loss and was now coming to the end of it.

"Well," he said casually as he shrugged the garment back on, seeming not to have been affected at all by their brief interlude. "Thanks for the use of your...facilities."

She expelled a soft, puzzled sound. "You didn't use my facilities," she reminded him.

He smiled in that intense, heat-inducing way again. "Didn't I? Oh. My mistake. I stand corrected."

Winona had no idea what to say in response to that, so she only kept silent.

"I can see myself out," he told her, grinning again.

"Yes, I daresay you can," she replied faintly.

He considered her again for a moment, once more seeming to focus his attention on her mouth. Then he turned around and exited her kitchen, without a single backward glance. She heard his muffled footfalls on the Oriental carpet that spanned her hallway, then the almost inaudible *thump-thump-thump* of his feet as he descended the stairs toward the restaurant. For long moments Winona only stood in her kitchen gazing out the door, wondering if she hadn't just dreamed the entire incident. Then she inhaled a deep breath and detected just the merest hint of his scent that had been left behind.

No, she hadn't dreamed it. Connor Montgomery was all too real. So now only one question remained. What on earth had just happened between them?

Holy Mary, Mother of God, Connor thought when he managed to make it back to his car in one piece. What the hell had just happened up there in Winona Thornbury's house? One minute, he'd been completely in charge of the situation, had known exactly what his next step would be, had, in fact, had Madam Winona right where he wanted her. In that minute, he had been *this* close to getting at least a couple of answers to the numerous questions floating around in his brain. And then the next minute...

Whoa.

The next minute, he'd had no idea what the hell he was doing, or where the hell he was—save some dizzying black hole of need and wanting, unlike anyplace he'd ever visited before. As he'd felt the rush of warm water streaming over his hand, he'd suddenly, as if from a very great distance, heard her murmur something in that soft, husky voice of hers. And when he'd glanced up from the sink, he'd found her gazing at him in a way he'd never seen a woman gazing at him before. Not a woman who was fully clothed, anyway. Damn, not even a woman who was naked and moaning and writhing beneath him had ever looked at him like that before.

But there had been Winona Thornbury, all buttoned up in that old-fashioned thing that hid every curve she had—well, as well as curves like that could be hidden—with her hair all neatly pinned around her head like some schoolmarm from the last century, looking as if she were about to come apart right there in her own kitchen. Her cheeks had been flushed, her full, lush lips had been slightly parted, her pupils had been expanded, and the pulse had been beating erratically at the base of her throat. She'd looked as if she were *that* close to going off.

And there had been Connor, ready to go off right behind her. Because the moment he'd seen her looking at him that way, he'd been hard as a rock and ready to roll. Never in his life had a hard-on come on that rapidly, or that fiercely.

It made no sense. Sure, Madam Winona was gorgeous and sexy and hot and luscious and delectable and... and...and... Where was he? Oh, yeah. Sure she was a sexy woman, but so were scores of other women in town. Connor was no stranger to looking at beautiful women—hey, what man was?—but something about gazing at Madam Winona had left him feeling hazy and stupid and helpless.

And *helpless* was a feeling Connor Monahan didn't like *at all.* He wasn't altogether fond of stupid or hazy, either.

Which was why he'd immediately had to step in and re-capture the upper hand, by stepping forward toward Madam Winona as if he intended to…to…to… Well, to do what came naturally. But that upper hand had eluded him for some time, because the nearer he'd drawn to Madam Winona, the hazier, stupider and more helpless he'd felt.

He still couldn't figure out what had happened, still didn't understand the torpor and fascination that had come over him just from gazing at her. She'd just looked so… And she'd made him feel so… And all he'd wanted to do was…

Holy Mary, Mother of God. He'd be better off not thinking about it.

And on top of that, he'd totally blown his chance to have a look around upstairs at the infamous Winona's, which had been what had lured him up there to begin with. When he'd seen that big party going up earlier in the evening, he'd realized he had an excuse for wandering up there himself later on, to have a little look around. So after he'd finished his dinner, he'd left the restaurant for a while, returning just before closing to tuck himself into a corner where no one would notice him. And then, when he'd seen Winona Thornbury climb the stairs, he'd realized his chance to get a better look at both her *and* her…facilities.

He'd been a little disappointed when her facilities had turned out to be what was clearly her private residence, filled with frilly, ornate antiques and flowered wallpaper and whimsical lamps and Persian rugs and other old, girly stuff. All in all, her decor hadn't been much to Connor's liking. He was a twenty-first-century guy of the first order, preferring clean lines and stark contrasts and few colors in his decorating schemes. Still, he supposed it shouldn't have come as a surprise that Winona's home would look like, well, a turn-of-the-century brothel. Nevertheless, he wished it had *been* a brothel. Sure would have saved him some time and trouble.

When he'd finally stumbled upon her, it hadn't been all that hard for him to play the ignorant dunce who had accidentally wandered into an area he wasn't supposed to be in. God knew he'd played the fool before—not so long ago, in fact—though it was definitely a role he hadn't relished, nor one he wanted to repeat. Still, Winona had fallen for it, hadn't she? She'd had no idea who he was or why he was in her house, except for having taken a misstep on his way to the men's room.

But Connor had completely messed up what was probably going to be his only chance to really investigate her digs, by fleeing in panic and confusion when he should have been pressing his advantage. Certainly he wished now he had pressed something in Madam Winona's kitchen. Like maybe Madam Winona herself. Yeah, like maybe he should have pressed her back against the counter there, even lifted her up on it to settle himself between her legs, thereby giving himself more freedom, freedom to run his hands up under her nightgown, over her bare calves and shins and knees and thighs, then higher still, to—

Enough, he told himself. He was just going to drive himself crazy if he kept this up.

And just why the hell *was* he keeping this up? he wondered wildly. Just what the hell *had* happened in there? Man. He really wasn't getting out enough. That much was obvious. Maybe he ought to call up that redhead on the Bloomington investigative team. What was her name? Lynette, that was it. Yeah, Lynette seemed much more his speed—fast.

Then again, how much faster could you get than a current-Madam-slash-former-pro? And why did Connor suddenly find it so hard to believe that Winona Thornbury was either? She *had* to be the ringleader of the prostitution operation, he told himself. There was no other explanation for it. How could any legitimate businesswoman not know what was going on under her own roof? Of course she was in on it. Of course she was the one in charge.

Even if she did still seem like a nice, old-fashioned girl. Even if no experienced woman blushed the way Winona Thornbury had blushed when Connor had suggested, none too subtly, that he wanted to make use of her facilities.

And what the hell kind of woman still used the word *daresay* in this day and age?

She was a puzzle all right, Connor thought as he turned the key in his ignition and heard the satisfying rumble of the little two-seater sports car's motor purring to life. A puzzle he couldn't wait to figure out. Because one thing was certain. Even if he'd blown his chance to get a better look around Madam Winona's digs, he still had every intention of getting a better look at Madam Winona herself.

Oh, yeah, he thought further as he sped out of the parking lot and into the busy street. He planned on being quite a regular at the restaurant for the next few nights. Maybe longer. At least as long as it took to uncover everything he needed to know. About Winona Thornbury's prostitution ring.

And about Winona Thornbury herself.

Three

—

Winona was thinking about how nice it was that Monday evenings were so slow, as if in apology for the velocity and insanity of the weekends, when her evening suddenly went haywire. And all because of a simple request relayed by one of her waiters.

"Winona," Teddy said as he poked his dark, shaggy head into the kitchen, where she was removing the last of her famous white-chocolate and raspberry tortes from the oven. "There's a gentleman sitting at table seventeen who's asked you to join him."

Her eyebrows shot up in surprise as she settled the confection gently on the counter, and she was certain her expression reflected the same astonishment that Teddy's did. "Don't you mean he's asked to *see* me?"

Teddy shook his head. "No, I mean he's asked you to *join* him. For dinner," he clarified further.

"But…but…but…"

Unfortunately, no other words except for that one, not

particularly polite one, would emerge from Winona's mouth. Certainly her patrons asked to speak with her from time to time, to ask about the menu selections or compliment her on one or two particular favorites. Once or twice she'd even had to field a minor complaint, though that, fortunately, was a very rare occurrence. However, none of her customers had ever asked Winona to join them, for dinner or anything else. What the man at table seventeen was requesting was quite unusual.

And if the man at table seventeen was who Winona suspected he was, what he was requesting was also quite exciting.

No, not exciting! she immediately admonished herself. It was unacceptable! *Completely* unacceptable. There was no way she would join *him*—for dinner or anything else.

"He was pretty adamant," Teddy added when Winona said nothing in response. "I mean, he was polite, but…you know…adamant."

Oh, yes, she could certainly believe that. After what had happened Friday night, Winona knew the man could be quite formidable. Among other things.

"Very well," she said softly, not knowing what else to do. She feared that if she didn't go out and at least talk to Mr. Montgomery, he might venture into the kitchen to find her. And the last thing she needed or wanted was for her staff to bear witness to…well…to whatever it was that seemed to burn up the air between the two of them whenever they were in the same room. It was unsettling enough that Winona had been witness to it herself.

Unsettling, she thought again. To put it mildly. She'd had trouble sleeping for the last three nights, thanks to Mr. Connor Montgomery. Because the moment she switched off her light and nestled herself under her covers, she was assailed by memories of him. Memories of how his heat had encircled her, of the deep, mellow timbre of his voice, of how handsome he was and how good he had smelled.

Memories of how very much she had wanted him, regardless of the mysterious origins of that desire.

And when she finally did fall asleep, it only grew worse. Because he invaded her dreams then, and, unconscious, Winona was helpless to stop those dreams from going too far. And in her dreams Connor Montgomery went beyond formidable. In her dreams he was relentless, towering over her, bending his head to hers, covering her mouth with his, his hands roaming over her entire, and often naked, body. In her dreams he said things to her, did things to her, that no man had ever said or done before. And in her dreams Winona, heaven help her, had only wanted him to do more.

Fortunately, upon waking in the morning, she had always been able to reclaim her sanity and good sense. She wasn't the wanton her dreams made her out to be. She was a decent, virtuous woman who had no room in her life for someone like Connor Montgomery. She'd allowed a man like him into her life before—completely ignorant of his wanton, licentious habits, of course—and had been left heartbroken as a result. She wasn't about to make the same mistake again. She wasn't about to have any more to do with Connor Montgomery than she absolutely had to.

"Tell him I, ah… I'll be right there," she said to Teddy, who nodded in response and disappeared back out into the restaurant.

Winona ran a quick hand over her hair, tucking a few errant strands of blond back into the chignon she had fashioned at her nape. Then she removed the apron she had tossed on over her calf-length, ruby-red dress—the one piped along the yolk and short sleeves with black velvet, boasting a black velvet collar and two dozen ebony buttons down the back. Then she inhaled a deep, steadying breath, and told herself not to panic.

She didn't have to actually *join* Mr. Montgomery for dinner, she told herself. She would simply explain to him how busy she was, regardless of it being a Monday night and the restaurant being nearly deserted, and he would just have to understand.

There. That was simple enough. It was settled.

Unfortunately, the moment Winona entered the dining room and saw Mr. Montgomery seated at table seventeen, she became decidedly *un*settled again. Oh, yes. Very unsettled indeed. Because his gaze immediately flew to hers and fixed itself there, and she was once more held in thrall by his intense blue eyes. And she realized then that nothing about her explanation would be simple at all. She'd count herself fortunate if she could remember even the most rudimentary vocabulary and enunciate her words clearly.

"Mr. Montgomery," she said as cheerfully as she could as she approached his table. "How nice to have you back at Winona's so soon. We must have made quite an impression on you the other night."

He smiled that wicked smile of his after she uttered the comment, which she realized, too late, carried a double entendre she hadn't intended for it to carry at all. Because had he taken one more step toward her in her kitchen on Friday night, he would have been making quite an impression on her indeed. One she sincerely doubted she would have forgotten.

"I mean, ah…" She began to backpedal.

But his low, meaningful chuckle halted her. Well, that, and the fact that she had no idea what to say to excuse her faux pas.

"Please, Miss Thornbury," he said softly, holding up a hand in a silent indication that she shouldn't even bother trying to explain. Probably, she thought, because he wouldn't believe her anyway. He swiveled his hand then to indicate the chair opposite his. "Join me for dinner."

Instead of sitting, Winona gripped the back of the chair with sure fingers and remained standing. "Thank you for the invitation," she said, her voice touched with irony, because Mr. Montgomery's edict had been anything *but* an invitation. "But I don't make a practice of joining my customers for meals. I'm much too busy."

"No exceptions?" he asked,

"No, I'm afraid not."

"Not even this once?"

"No. Thank you."

"Not even if I told you I can't stop thinking about what happened Friday night?"

Oh, dear…

"Mr. Montgomery—"

"Please, call me Connor."

"Mr. Montgomery," she reiterated, more forcefully than before, "I'm afraid that what happened Friday night—"

"And just what did happen Friday night, Miss Thornbury?" he interrupted. Again. "Have you figured it out? Because I thought about it an awful lot this weekend, and I'll be damned if I can even begin to understand."

Oh, dear, she thought. He had felt it, too. "I'm not sure I know what you mean," she said evasively.

"Oh, I think you know exactly what I mean."

"I—" She halted right there. This was nonsense. He was starting to behave like a teenager—which shouldn't come as a surprise, she supposed, seeing as how he hadn't aged much beyond the decade in question. And she wanted no part of such a thing. So she looked him squarely in the eye and told him, "Thank you again for the invitation, Mr. Montgomery. Have a nice evening. I hope dinner meets with your approval."

And with that, she spun on her heel and began to walk away. She was feeling rather smug, thinking she'd handled the situation fairly well, all things considered, when she felt confident fingers circling her upper arm, urging her to turn around. The gesture was punctuated by a softly uttered, "Winona, wait."

The gentle timbre of his voice surprised her, and hearing him utter her first name in such a way set her off-kilter. As a result, she stumbled a bit as she pivoted around. But Mr. Montgomery caught her other arm capably in his free hand to steady her. And then she stood face-to-face with him again—well, as face-to-face as one could stand to someone whose height was so…enhanced. But she was gazing into his beautiful blue eyes again, marveling at the fire she saw burning in their depths. Marveling, too, at the shiver of delight that shuddered through her at hearing him address her the way he had. And wondering at the tingle of heat that seeped through her sleeves where his hands were curved over her arms.

"Please wait," he repeated, even more softly than before. And then, even more surprisingly, he added, "I apologize. I suppose I was out of line."

"Yes," she agreed, every bit as softly. "You were."

"I'm sorry if I said something that offended you," he told her again. "I promise I'll behave myself if you'll agree to join me for dinner."

"And as I told you, Mr. Montgomery—"

"Connor."

"Mr. Montgomery, I don't join my customers for dinner. I'm even less obliged to join them for suggestive banter. I'd thank you to keep yours to yourself."

He said nothing for a moment, only continued to gaze down at her face, as if he couldn't quite make sense of what he beheld there. Then, "I really haven't been able to stop thinking about Friday night," he told her. "You're a haunting woman, Winona."

Again, her name on his lips. Again the shudder of heat that wound through her. Again the memories of Friday night assailing her. Winona closed her eyes for a moment, thinking maybe the gesture would help her drive them all away. But when she opened her eyes again, when she saw Connor Montgomery's face so close to her own, when she felt his heat, inhaled his scent…

"All right," she said. "I suppose it won't hurt to join you this once."

And she absolutely could not *believe* she had said what she had said. She simply did not join her patrons for meals. It wasn't professional. It breached the rules of etiquette. It blurred the line between social stations. Winona was a firm believer in all of these things. Yet she had just disregarded all of them for the sake of—

What? she wondered. What was she hoping to gain by having dinner with Connor Montgomery?

When he smiled at her again, she began to get an inkling of an answer to her own question. But she battled back the tide of pleasure that swelled inside her and reminded herself this was *not* a personal endeavor. No, she was only doing this because…because…because…

Well, just because. That was why. And it was a perfectly good reason, too.

Having justified—however feebly—her intentions, Winona allowed herself to be guided back to table seventeen, which, she recalled now, was one of their more romantically positioned tables. It was shaded on one side by a fat potted palm, by the fireplace on another and by a silk screen on a third side. The effect, on the whole, was one of seclusion and privacy—as secluded and private as one might get in a public building, at any rate.

In a surprising display of courtesy, Mr. Montgomery pulled out her chair for her, waited for her to be seated, then scooted her back toward the table. Then he seated himself directly opposite and reached for an opened bottle of red wine. Immediately Winona covered her glass with her palm, but he deftly moved it away, and, disregarding her silent protest, filled her glass with the ruby liquid before topping off his own. Then he sat back in his chair and eyed her with much interest, twirling his glass gently by the stem.

"So," he said. "What shall we talk about?"

Winona fingered the stem of her own glass, but didn't lift it. "I have no idea, Mr. Montgomery. You're the one who…invited…me to join you. In a manner of speaking," she couldn't keep herself from adding. "I assumed you had a specific topic in mind."

"Oh, I do," he assured her, smiling again. "But you won't let me talk about what I want to talk about. You run away when I bring it up."

She gaped faintly at him. "I did *not* run away."

"Didn't you?"

She straightened in her chair, her back going stiff, her derriere perched daintily on the very edge of her seat. "Certainly not," she told him imperiously.

"Hoo-kay," he told her, smiling in a way that indicated he didn't for one second believe her. "If you say so."

"I do."

He smiled again, then enjoyed a generous taste of his wine. "You're not from around here originally, are you?" he asked suddenly.

She arched her eyebrows at the swift change of subject. "Actually, I've been living in Bloomington since I came here to attend college twenty years ago."

His expression changed drastically then. "You went to college twenty years ago?" he echoed incredulously. "You're that… Uh, I mean… Ah…"

"Yes, Mr. Montgomery," she said, battling a smile— not to mention a few social conventions— "I'm that old."

"I didn't mean—"

"Didn't you?" she asked, taking perverse pleasure in being the one to interrupt him and set him off-kilter this time.

"No, I just… I meant… I mean… It's just that… Well, you sure don't look…"

Winona could scarcely believe it. She'd left him speechless. She had him feeling awkward. Well, my, my, my. Wasn't he just a bundle of surprises.

"Thank you," she said, sparing him from further discomfort. "I think."

He gazed at her for a few more minutes, as if he were looking for something, though she knew not what. Then, seeming satisfied with his perusal, he continued, "So... where are you from originally?"

"I grew up in Indianapolis with my sister, Miriam, and a maiden aunt who raised us."

Mr. Montgomery narrowed his eyes at her, as if in confusion. "Maiden aunt?" he repeated.

"Yes. Is there a problem with that?"

He shook his head. "No, it's just... I don't think I've ever heard the phrase 'maiden aunt' in, oh...my entire life."

"You heard it just now," Winona pointed out.

This time he nodded. But he seemed no less confused. "Yeah. I guess so. Gee, new experiences happen everyday, don't they?"

More was the pity, Winona couldn't help thinking. Oh, to be able to turn back time, she thought further, and to live in an age when things were so much simpler. Especially things between men and women. There had been specific roles back then, specific expectations, specific boundaries. None of the parry and thrust and ups and downs and confusing shades of gray that were so inherent in modern romantic relationships.

Of course, had she lived in those times, she probably wouldn't have been able to own her own business, she reminded herself. And she wouldn't have had the freedom to come and go as she liked, the way she did now. She wouldn't have been able to vote. Wouldn't have been allowed to own property. She would, no doubt, have been obligated, or even forced, to marry a man she didn't love. She may well have died in childbirth.

Oh, all *right,* she thought. So there were one or two things to be said for modern times. She just wished there could be more things said for modern relationships. Because Winona wasn't equipped to handle those. The one time she had tried, she had ended up with a broken heart. She wasn't about to wander into another one. Especially with a thoroughly modern man like Connor Montgomery.

"Really, Mr. Montgomery," she said, "if all you want is my biography, I can drop one in the mail to you tomorrow. As much as I appreciate your interest, I have work that I really should be doing, and—"

"Look, I'm going about this all wrong," he said, interrupting her. *Again.* "I just... I want to get to know you better, and I thought this might be the best way. You don't seem to take any time off from your job here."

He'd noticed? she thought, not certain whether that was a good thing or a bad thing. "Well, one does have to fairly well devote one's life to a new business, until it's well established, doesn't one?" she said.

"Yours looks pretty well established," he remarked.

And why did his voice carry such a wry tone when he said it? she wondered.

"I don't want to get complacent," she told him.

"I'll just bet you don't," he replied, in that odd tone of voice again.

Winona stood. She had no idea what Mr. Montgomery's game was, but even someone as unsophisticated as she in the give-and-take of men and women could sense that there was something fishy going on. And she wanted no part of it. Whatever it was.

"If you'll excuse me, Mr. Montgomery, I just remembered something very important I need to attend to right away."

"What's that?" he asked, clearly suspicious of her withdrawal.

"My good sense," she told him. There. Let him make of that what he would. Before he had the chance to pursue her comment—or her—Winona spun quickly around. Then, as much as she hated to admit it—she ran away.

Connor knew he was skirting the edge of ethical behavior—among other things—by trying to wheedle his way into Winona Thornbury's private life the way he had Friday night and again tonight. But he was so frustrated after so many weeks of hitting nothing but dead ends that he had arrived at, well, his wit's end. He'd worry about ethics later, he told himself as he watched her flee the scene. He would. At some point. Before it was too late. Probably. Right now, though, he had an illegal operation to break up, and he was determined to do it any way he knew how.

And he was still thinking about that later that evening, as he sat in an unmarked police car parked discreetly in the alley behind Winona's. But he also realized he was having a whole lot of trouble focusing on the illegal operation and his determination. Because all he could think about as he sat in that darkened car was the way Winona Thornbury had looked earlier that evening when she was seated across his table, as she'd told him a few rudimentary things about her past.

Naturally, Connor had already known most of those things about her past, because he'd read the police report the Bloomington PD had run on her as part of the investigation. He'd known when he went upstairs Friday that Winona lived above her restaurant—that had been the main reason he'd gone up there. In a word, duh.

Well, he'd gone up there for that, and also to see if maybe there was some kind of wild, illegal orgy going on in one of the rooms, with cash passing hands freely in exchange for deviant sexual behavior, and Winona ringing up unlawful acts on a cash register, one by illicit one. Hey, you never knew. He could luck into something like that. It wasn't outside the realm of possibility.

And he also knew that she'd lived in a small studio apartment three blocks away before opening Winona's, knew that she'd moved to Bloomington some time ago, knew she was a graduate of IU and that she had worked in a variety of restaurants in town before opening her own, knew she had no prior arrest record—not that that meant anything. Ted Bundy hadn't had a prior arrest record, either, and look how that had turned out.

But Connor hadn't paid much attention to specific dates in the police report as he'd scanned it, save those that pertained to the investigation itself. So Winona Thornbury's age, if nothing else, had come as a total surprise to him. She didn't look like a woman in her late thirties, no way. He would have pegged her in her late twenties, at most. Certainly he wouldn't have guessed that she was more than a few years beyond his own, recently acquired, twenty-nine.

Wow. Her sexual history must *really* be impressive, seeing as how she had almost a full decade on him.

Still, what difference did it make that she was nine or ten years older than him? he asked himself. It wasn't like he was interested in her. And hell, even if he was interested in her, he wasn't going to let a little thing like age difference come between them. Connor Monahan never let anything come between him and a beautiful woman. The less there was between them, the better, as a matter-of-fact— both literally and figuratively.

Still, he couldn't stop thinking about Winona.

He told himself it was only because she was so central to the investigation. Unfortunately, he wasn't very good at convincing himself of that. Because he was reasonably sure that the fact that she smelled like fresh lilacs after a summer rain wasn't integral to whether or not she was the leader of a prostitution ring. And neither was the fact that her skin had looked creamier and softer than a baby's tushie. And neither was the fact that her full, dewy lips looked sweeter than pink cotton candy.

Snap out of it, Monahan, he told himself. This is getting

you nowhere. Except more frustrated. Plus, it's embarrassing to see a grown man going on that way.

"You better be careful, Monahan," his borrowed partner, Glenn Davison, said from the passenger seat. He blew over the edge of a huge throwaway cup—one that, for non-caffeine addicts, might potentially hold a week's worth of coffee. "Calling her to your table tonight…that was pretty sloppy. Cap'n's gonna be ticked off about that when he hears."

"Yeah, yeah, yeah," Connor muttered. "I was just putting out some feelers—so to speak. We're getting nowhere on this case."

Davison snorted his derision in response to that. "Yeah, well, it's one thing to be feelin' a woman. It's another to get your ass hauled in on entrapment. If I were you, I'd be more careful."

"You're not me," Connor said simply, grateful for that particular reality. Although he didn't know his temporary partner well, Glenn Davison seemed to be the kind of man who wasn't into what most men were into. Like tidy dressing habits, for one thing. Like good dental hygiene for another. Or any hygiene, for that matter. As unobtrusively as he could, Connor rolled down his window a bit.

Hell, he shouldn't even be working on this case, he reminded himself. He was a member of the Marigold, Indiana, Police Department, forty-five minutes away. But the Bloomington boys had discovered during the course of their investigation that the girls working Winona's came not only from all walks of life, but all parts of the state, as well. It was yet another reason why they suspected that at least some of the girls were students.

There was even a girl from Connor's hometown of Marigold who had been working as a highly placed hooker in the organization. And that was something he simply could not abide. His hometown was one of the last vestiges of small-town life left in America, free of crime, free of poverty, free of strife. Hell, pretty much free of reality, truth be told. But he intended to do everything in his power to keep it that way.

Simply put, Marigold, Indiana was a "nice place." But not only was a Marigold girl tied up with the Bloomington prostitution ring, there were good indications from Connor's own investigation back home that she intended to start up a similar operation in Marigold. When his local investigation of her had overlapped the Bloomington PD's, they'd somehow found themselves all working together. Which was how he'd ended up with Davison as his current partner, and the Budget Motor Lodge, Bloomington, as his temporary home.

Damned bad luck.

"All I'm sayin'," Davison began again, after a couple of messy slurps of his coffee, "is that you better make sure you do this by the book. Cap'n's already steamed enough that you're even on this case."

"Yeah, well, that wasn't my idea, was it? Your chief called mine and insisted."

"Anyway, if I were you, I'd make damned sure I didn't do anything to compromise this investigation. You don't know Cap'n like I do."

"And as I already pointed out," Connor said, "you're not me."

He was about to elaborate, gleefully pointing out the many differences between himself and Davison, but his attention was diverted when a light came on upstairs at Winona's. Their vantage point in the car was far too angled for Connor to do much more than note the illumination, but he gazed up at that light as if it were the Holy Grail, in spite of his inability to see into the brightened room.

He knew her office was on the front side of the building, because he'd seen it during his brief foray into her humble abode. And although he hadn't pinpointed the location of her bedroom—he hadn't been able to make it that far before stumbling upon her in her kitchen—he decided the window at which he gazed now more than likely opened into that very room. Madam Winona would probably call it her *boudoir,* in that old-fashioned way of hers. To Connor's way of thinking, though, it was more along the lines of, oh…he didn't know. The words *pleasure dome* came to mind.

For long moments he only stared at the open window from which that pale-yellow light spilled, his mind's eye entertaining all sorts of possible scenarios that might be unfolding there. Winona striding into the room, her hands lifted to the scores of buttons that had fastened her dress earlier, unfastening them one by leisurely one, then shrugging the garment off her shoulders, pushing it down over her hips and thighs, tossing it onto a chair in the corner.

Beneath it, she no doubt wore some kind of nineteenth-century underwear, something manufactured of white cotton and whalebone, decorated with satin ribbons and frilly lace, with more buttons going down the front. Every time Connor got a load of Winona and her buttons, he was overcome by the desire—nay, the very need—to undo them all himself, one by leisurely one.

Don't think about it, Monahan, he cautioned himself. You'll just make yourself crazy.

And then she'd probably go to work on those buttons herself, he couldn't help continuing his mental picture, loosing each one with those delicate fingers of hers. Little by little the white fabric would open, revealing the dusky valley between her breasts, her ivory torso, her flat belly, the dimple of her navel. Then more, toward—

Connor squeezed his eyes shut tight and somehow willed his imagination to curb its wildly overwrought workings. He had to get a grip on himself. This was insane. There was no reason why he should be so fascinated by Winona Thornbury. No rational reason, at any rate. Hell, she wasn't even anything like the women he normally dated. He usually went for women who were sophisticated and modern, women who didn't use words like *daresay* and *maiden aunt.* He went for women who wore miniskirts and platform shoes and thong underwear, not whalebone and lace and buttons. Oh, and one more thing. He also tended to go for women who were *not* the leaders of prostitution rings.

That was it, he finally realized. That was the secret to Winona Thornbury's allure. She presented a paradox that no one with a Y chromosome could resist. Old-fashioned, prim and proper on the outside, a raging conflagration of coitus and debauchery on the inside. Every man's wildest sexual fantasies disguised as an innocent naïf. Virgin and whore in one convenient package. What man wouldn't be fascinated by that?

Just as the thought formed in Connor's brain, Winona Thornbury herself appeared at the open window, to push the sash down a bit, and to loosen a tie that held back one lacy panel. Connor's lips parted involuntarily as he homed in on what should have been an unremarkable action, one that lasted only a few seconds. He couldn't help it. He was stunned.

Because she *had* been dressed in a white cotton underthing decorated with satin ribbons and frilly lace. And as she'd freed the curtain, she had been unfastening the scores of buttons with her free hand, one by leisurely one. He had, for one scant instant, beheld the dusky valley between her breasts. And as the lace had fallen over the window, over Winona, obscuring her from his view, his mind's eye had seen again—all too clearly—exactly what he was missing.

And oh, boy. Was he missing a lot.

"This is gettin' us nowhere," Davison said then, dispelling Connor's licentious ruminations. "I don't know what you were hopin' to learn by staking out the place tonight, anyway. I told you we've done this before, probably a half-dozen times already, and we got nothin' from it. I told you this was gonna net you a big fat zero."

"Not quite a zero," Connor said, still gazing at the window from which Winona had disappeared. He had, after all, learned something very important. He'd learned that Winona Thornbury was every bit as lush and luscious as he had thought.

And he had learned it was going to be very, *very* difficult for him to bring her in. Not just because she was so elusive. But because he very much suspected that once he had her in his possession, he wasn't ever going to want to let her go.

Four

What followed Monday night felt, to Winona, like a veritable blitzkrieg of Connor Montgomery. Because he came into the restaurant every night that week. And he invited her to join him for dinner every night that week. And when she turned down his invitation—every night that week—he stayed late at the bar after finishing his meal. Every night that week. And he was still there at closing every night that week. She had to virtually chase him out of her establishment every night that week.

Or, more correctly, she had to ask whichever host or hostess was on duty that night to chase him out of her establishment every night that week. Because there was no way that Winona would get any closer to the man than she had to. *Any* night that week.

And that was due to the fact that every night that week he was dressed in his usual breathtakingly handsome way. Every night his blue eyes shone bewitchingly, and his full mouth crooked up playfully at the corners as if he knew something she didn't. Every night he became more and more overpowering, and more and more irresistible. And every time she turned down his invitation to dinner, Winona felt a curl of disappointment wind through her. But every time she turned him down, he became even more adamant when issuing his next invitation. And invariably her ensuing disappointment became even more keen.

By Saturday night she was at her wit's end. She simply could not understand why the man would spend so much time at the restaurant, or why he would continue to ask her to join him for dinner when she had made it abundantly clear that she wasn't interested. And she continued to not understand it on Saturday, when Connor Montgomery corralled her by the host stand just prior to closing and asked her, point-blank, "If you won't join me for dinner in your own restaurant, then how about joining me for dinner at someone else's?"

And then Winona had no idea what to say. Except maybe for, "I, ah…um…er…that is…ahem…oh…" Or stammerings to that effect.

Stammerings that must have been amusing to him for some reason, because the more discomfited she became, the broader his smile grew. "C'mon, Winona," he said. "Let me take you to dinner. You deserve a night off once in a while. All work and no play…"

"Makes for a very successful business," she quickly finished for him. Anything to change the subject.

But Mr. Montgomery was clearly resistant to such a change. "Yeah, but if you keep up at this rate, you're going to burn out. And burnout always leads to disaster." He smiled that toe-curling smile again. "C'mon," he murmured again. "Just one evening. Just one dinner. Where's the harm in that?"

The harm, Winona knew, was standing right there in front of her—six-feet-plus of raw, virile jeopardy. Connor Montgomery, she was certain, could very well be the death of her. And not in some sociopathic, serial killer sense, either. But simply because he was too handsome, too charming, too sexy, too modern, too confident, too masculine, too…too…

Just *too*. That was all. And that was a *very* big problem.

"Thank you, Mr. Montgomery—"

"Connor."

"Mr. Montgomery, but I really can't," she told him.

"Monday would be good," he countered immediately, as if he hadn't heard her. "How about Monday? This place seems to be pretty slow on Mondays. You could sneak off for a few hours."

She arched her eyebrows in surprise. "A few hours? Well, my goodness, Mr. Montgomery. Just how long do you plan on dinner taking?"

"Oh, dinner should only take an hour or so," he told her with much confidence. But he didn't elaborate, beyond smiling that devilishly wicked smile of his.

"I see," she said coolly. "Thank you. No."

His impish smile fell some then, and his arrogant posture eased. He expelled a long, weary breath and ran a restless hand through his dark hair. "Look, I'm sorry. What if I promise to be a perfect gentleman on Monday night?"

Winona couldn't quite prevent the chuckle that escaped her. Nor could she quite keep herself from replying, as politely as she could, "Oh, Mr. Montgomery, I sincerely doubt that."

His smile shone one thousand watts again. "You doubt that I would make that promise?" he asked. "Or you doubt that I could be a perfect gentleman?"

Winona weighed her answer carefully. There were times, she knew, when honesty had no place in courtesy. Yet she was the most honest, courteous person she knew. She strove to be honest and courteous above all else. Oh, dear. A dilemma. A paradox. What to do, what to do…

In the end honesty won out. Probably because she imagined Mr. Montgomery would appreciate that quality over courtesy. "I don't think you can be a perfect gentleman," she said respectfully. "It's nothing personal, mind you. I just don't think that chivalry is at the top of your to-do list, that's all. It's a problem that plagues many members of your generation."

That, too, made him smile. "My generation isn't so far off from your generation," he told her.

"That's what you think," she replied. "*I'm* not a member of my generation."

He narrowed his eyes at her, clearly puzzled. "What do you mean?"

But Winona only smiled in response. How could she adequately explain her old-fashioned tendencies to a man who was so firmly rooted in the here and now?

No explanation seemed necessary, however, because Mr. Montgomery nodded his comprehension. "Oh, I get it. You think you were born a few generations too late. That's why you dress the way you do and use words like *daresay*."

"Something like that, yes," she agreed.

"Still, Winona, even the most old-fashioned girls have one or two modern…needs. You can still be an old-fashioned girl and get…dated."

Winona feigned indifference to his suggestive remark, but she felt a ripple of heat undulate right down her spine. It was simply another indication as to why she shouldn't be anywhere near this man. All he would do was compromise her. Old-fashioned, indeed. "Do they? Can they?" she finally asked. "I wouldn't know."

But he only eyed her expectantly. "I'll bet you know more than you're letting on."

"Mr. Montgomery—"

"I can be a perfect gentleman, Winona," he interjected before she had a chance to say anything more. But he began to smile that naughty smile again, and she wasn't quite sure how to take his remark. "And I'll prove it to you. Have dinner with me Monday. If I'm not a perfect gentleman, then I promise I'll never bother you again."

Now that, Winona thought, was a proposition that interested her very much indeed. The thought of coming in to work without having Connor Montgomery watching her every move was really very…very…very… How odd. For some reason, the idea that he might stop coming in to Winona's once and for all brought with it a strange feeling of melancholy.

Oh, fiddle-faddle, Winona told herself. She was being silly. Coming to work without having Connor Montgomery there bothering her would make her life infinitely easier. She was more than a little tempted to take him up on his offer. Only to stop him from bothering her, of course. Because she was confident that there was no way he could behave himself as a perfect gentleman all evening. Even though she didn't know the man well, she could see that gallantry simply wasn't in his nature.

She considered him thoughtfully for a moment as she weighed the pros and cons of his proposition. "You won't pester me to join you for dinner here at the restaurant anymore?" she asked.

He shook his head.

"You won't waste my time calling me to your table so that you can indulge me in frivolous banter and insinuative innuendo?"

"No frivolous banter," he promised. "No, um, insinuative, ah…innuendo."

She eyed him thoughtfully for a moment more, until his good looks, devilish grin and sparkling blue eyes nearly overwhelmed her. "Do I have your word on that?" she asked as she turned her gaze back down to the reservations book on the host stand.

"My word as a gentleman," he told her.

She chuckled again. "How about giving me your word

as a rogue instead?'' she asked. ''I think that would probably be more trustworthy.''

When she glanced up again, it was to find him studying her with much interest. ''Fine,'' he said with a reverent dip of his head. ''You have my word as a rogue. It's as good as gold.''

''Yes, I daresay it is,'' she said quietly. And, for some reason, her comment made him smile again. ''All right,'' she finally told him. ''I'll have dinner with you, Mr. Montgomery, on Monday night. At an establishment other than my own.''

Now his grin turned positively wicked, and his blue eyes blazed with something almost otherworldly.

Winona narrowed her eyes at him. ''A *commercial* establishment other than my own,'' she emphasized.

His smile fell some. But he quickly rallied it again. ''Fine,'' he said. ''We can do that. What time Monday?''

She thought for a moment more. Mondays truly were slow at the restaurant. She could add another host to the mix—Laurel again, because the girl was amazingly efficient—and things should move just swimmingly. At the restaurant, at any rate. With Mr. Montgomery, however...

Well. Winona reminded herself again that there was very little chance he would behave like a gentleman, perfect or imperfect. And the moment he erred, the moment he said something he shouldn't say or touched a part of her he had no business touching, she would call an immediate halt to the evening and demand that he escort her home. And that, once and for all, should put an end to his...whatever it was he wanted from her.

''How about seven o'clock?'' she finally said.

''No problem,'' he told her. ''I'll be here at seven on the dot.'' But he punctuated the remark with a lascivious look, one that sent more heat shimmering through Winona from head to toe.

Oh, yes, she thought, considering his expression once

again. There was no chance that Connor Montgomery would *ever* behave himself. She was as good as rid of him.

It occurred to Connor as he rang the bell at the side entrance of Winona's—the one that led to her private residence, instead of the restaurant—that even the outside of her house seemed like something from a long-ago age. A white picket fence—a *white picket fence,* he marveled again—edged the yard along the sidewalk, and its gate had creaked in happy welcome as he'd opened and passed through it. A cobbled walkway bisected a garden buzzing with all sorts of insect life, a garden that nearly overwhelmed him with the mingling and narcotic aromas of lilies and lilacs and lavender. There was a small bench, perfect for two, nestled against the side of the white frame house, beckoning him to sit with someone special after dark and murmur sweet nothings—yes, sweet nothings, dammit—into that someone special's ears.

Man, he was really losing it, he thought. Not only was he skirting the edge of ethical behavior, but he was actually, well, stopping to smell the lilacs. And that wasn't like Connor Monahan *at all.*

Hoo-boy, was he in it deep now, he thought further as he awaited a response to his summons at Winona's door. Not only had he promised something tonight that he was reasonably certain was impossible for him to deliver—that he would behave like a perfect gentleman—but he was in violation, he was sure, of every ethical rule in the "How Not To Screw Up an Investigation" handbook, which he had somehow missed receiving when he was bumped up to detective. Probably, he thought, he had been in the men's room shooting dice when they handed the book out.

Yeah, that was his story, and he was sticking to it.

Of course, he'd be telling Madam Winona another story entirely tonight. All about how he was just a lonesome, solitary businessman who was new in town, a lonely guy with money to burn and no one to burn it on, because he didn't know a single soul, and gosh, it was just so nice to be out with someone for a change, and gee, wouldn't it be nice if he could just pick up the phone sometime and make arrangements like this and have a charming, beautiful dinner companion like Winona every night of the week—and damn the expense, anyway.

There. That was nice and vague—and not entrapmenty at all to Connor's way of thinking. And it was gentlemanly, too, dammit. But it was also still open enough that she could reply with something along the lines of, "Well, you know, Mr. Montgomery, I just so happen to know of a company that provides such a companion, and for a reasonable fee, too, and we take all major credit cards, and here's our list of services all spelled out in writing and their corresponding charges, and…"

Hey, it could happen, he told himself.

When there was no reply to his summons, Connor extended one hand to ring the bell again while he used the other to fiddle with his pale-blue silk necktie. He'd chosen his navy-blue suit tonight, because he'd been told a couple of times that it complemented the color of his eyes just so nicely. Mushy talk, to be sure, but he wasn't taking any chances. He wanted to bring Madam Winona to her knees tonight, to put it incredibly crassly—and not a little Freudianly, he couldn't help thinking further.

The thought was still lingering in his mind when the door opened inward and there stood the object of his, uh…the object of his, um…of his, ah…and there stood Winona Thornbury, on the other side. And as always he was astounded by the utter purity of her beauty.

Tonight, as usual, she looked as if she had just stepped out of the early twentieth century. Her pale-blond hair was swept up in the back, knotted atop her head by some invisible means of support, interwoven with tiny white, sweet-smelling flowers he was certain were real. Her dress was white, too, an amazing confection comprised of layers of lacy…stuff, and satiny…stuff, and sheer…stuff, and embroidered…stuff, and—dammit—pearly buttons. The garment fell to midcalf above white, ankle-high boots with—surprise, surprise—more buttons anchoring her down.

And gloves, he noted with surprise. She was wearing white cotton gloves that buttoned—of course—at her wrists, leaving her arms bare up to the lacy cuffs of her elbow-length sleeves. And for some very strange reason he couldn't begin to understand, Connor found those gloves, and that stretch of bare, ivory arm, to be the sexiest thing he'd ever seen in his life.

God, he had to start getting out more.

"Good evening, Mr. Montgomery," she greeted him softly. "So nice of you to be on time."

He nodded. "Pretty gentlemanly of me, wasn't it?"

"Oh, yes," she told him. "Quite."

"Is it okay for me to say you look beautiful? Or would that be too forward?"

It stunned him to see a patch of pink bloom on each of her cheeks, as if what he'd just told her honestly embarrassed her. Her. A woman who'd take a man around the world for eighty bucks. Okay, probably a lot more than eighty bucks, he quickly amended. But, hell, it would be worth every penny.

"No," she said. "I don't believe that would be too forward. Not in this day and age."

"Then you look beautiful, Miss Winona."

When she glanced up, she was smiling at him, a sparkle of something Connor couldn't quite identify making her blue eyes seem as rich and limitless as a summer sky. Something fierce and fast hit him hard right in the solar plexus, but for the life of him, he couldn't say what it was—other than powerful. And all he could do was smile back at her and hope he didn't look as goofy as he felt.

Somewhere he found the intelligence to crook his arm

toward her and dip his head in a silent bid for her to loop her own arm through his. "Shall we go?" he asked further, in the most gentlemanly voice he could muster. "I thought that since it's such a nice evening, we might walk to our destination. It's not far."

She pulled the door closed softly behind her, locked it up, then deftly threaded her arm loosely through his. "That sounds lovely, Mr. Montgomery," she told him. "By all means, do lead on."

Winona tried to keep her eyes forward as she and Mr. Montgomery strolled down the street toward the Garden Path Café, where he had said they would be dining. She had no idea how he'd done it, but he'd managed to select her second-favorite restaurant in town—well, what kind of proprietress would she be if she didn't choose her *own* restaurant as her favorite?

The Garden Path Café was located on the street level of a quaint little bed and breakfast called, well, the Garden Path Bed and Breakfast. Not surprisingly, it was decorated in perfect harmony with its name—rose trellis wallpaper, hand-hooked rugs in floral patterns spanning the hardwood floors, scores of blossoming plants cascading from baskets that hung from the ceiling and scores of more blossoming plants springing from terra-cotta urns settled all about the floor.

But best of all, the restaurant was quiet and slow paced and in no way demanding. It was perfect for getting-to-know-you type conversation and little else. There would be scant opportunity for Mr. Montgomery to indulge in sly remarks or stolen touches. Contrary to tradition, in this case, Mr. Montgomery was being a true gentleman for leading Winona to the Garden Path.

Which was all the more reason why she tried to keep her eyes forward as they walked toward the café. He looked far too handsome and was behaving much too courteously for her comfort. He made chitchat of the most benign form as they strode slowly toward their destination, complimenting her on her garden, remarking on the beauty of the sunset, soliciting her opinion on *The Scarlet Pimpernel,* as he had just started reading it himself the day before.

In other words, he was being a perfect gentleman. And the realization of such a thing distressed Winona greatly. The last thing she needed or wanted was for Mr. Montgomery to behave himself politely. Because the last thing she needed or wanted was to be attracted to him more than she was already. As it was, she was struggling with some odd fascination with him, and she couldn't understand why she had been completely unable to quell it. She didn't want to make it worse by finding him so captivating. So charming. So...gallant.

It made no sense, why she should be so enthralled by a man such as he in the first place. He was her opposite in virtually every way, and he claimed none of the most fundamental qualities she desired in a man. Yet memories of him compromised her every waking moment, invading her thoughts, her dreams, her very life. She had been relieved that such a great social—and yes, age—chasm lay between the two of them, because she had thought they would never be able to span it. Now, however...

She sighed fretfully. Now she was beginning to think that the two of them might perhaps have more in common than she originally realized. And that would only lead to trouble. Because, regardless of their present camaraderie, Winona had the feeling that Mr. Montgomery wasn't a forever-after kind of man.

He clearly still had too much growing to do—both in chronological and psychological terms—before he could make that kind of commitment. He was too young, too impulsive, too *au courant* for the kind of old-fashioned pledge of marriage that she wanted herself. Yes, he might very well commit himself temporarily—to exactly the kind of physical relationship Winona wanted to avoid—but he was obviously not yet ready to settle down in any matrimonial sense.

And Winona demanded nothing less than at least *potential* matrimony from any man with whom she might pursue a personal relationship. She wasn't about to involve herself with a man unless he could approach their relationship with the intention of possibly marrying, just as she would approach it herself. If that meant she remained single for the rest of her life, then so be it. There were worse things in life, she knew, than living alone. One worse thing was falling in love, giving oneself utterly and completely to a man, and then having that man betray and abandon one.

She should know, after all. It had happened to her.

When Winona Thornbury fell, she fell irrevocably. There had only been one man in her life to whom she had given herself sexually. And she had only done so after the two of them had been dating for three years and engaged for eight months and were just three weeks shy of their wedding date. And although she had found such a... succumbing...to be quite, well, nice, actually—certainly nice enough to let it happen several times over the weeks that ensued—she wasn't about to fall prey to her carnal desires again. Not until she had a solid gold band solidly circling the fourth finger on her left hand.

She would not compromise herself or her virtue in such a way again. Because once her fiancé had enjoyed her...her...her... Well, once he had enjoyed *her,* he hadn't felt the need to stay around for very long. Only two weeks later she'd awoken one morning to find a note from him in her mailbox and him completely gone. And his hastily dashed-off letter had only driven home, painfully, just how foolish a woman she had been.

That was why Winona couldn't let herself fall under Connor Montgomery's spell. Even after such brief intercourse with him—for frightful lack of a better word—she could see that he was the kind of man who would be quick to seduce, slow to satisfy...and gone in sixty seconds. And Winona was the kind of woman who, once seduced and satisfied, would be forever under his spell. She'd had enough trouble pining over her lost fiancé—not that she really pined that much for Stanley Wadsworth these days. Nevertheless, she would be foolish to add another lost lover to the mix.

She told herself that wasn't likely to be a problem and that she was worrying for nothing, because Mr. Montgomery was bound to stumble over dinner. He couldn't possibly have the table manners necessary for polite society, and with the first misstep, he would cease to be a gentleman and he would thereafter be obliged to leave her alone.

But once they arrived at the café, he surprised her again, holding her chair for her as she seated herself, ordering considerately for both of them—after consulting her about her choice first, of course. He chose exactly the right wine, used the proper fork at the proper time... He even knew correct napkin ritual. It was astonishing.

"You've been studying this weekend," she charged lightly after their server had left them to their tea and coffee and cheesecake.

When Mr. Montgomery glanced up from his cup, his expression indicated that he was genuinely mystified by her statement. *As if,* Winona thought. To put it in the vulgar, contemporary vernacular.

"Studying?" he echoed innocently. "For what? No one told me there was going to be a test."

She smiled as she stirred milk into her tea. "Oh, come now, Mr. Montgomery. You knew full well going into this evening that you were going to be tested."

He smiled back. "Am I passing?"

"That," she said, feigning primness—for truly, she was beginning to feel less and less prim around him, "remains to be seen. The night is still young."

"So it is."

She would have expected one of his more lascivious grins to punctuate the comment, but he only turned his attention—very politely, drat him—back to his coffee.

"So, Mr. Montgomery, tell me a bit about yourself," Winona said after a dainty sip of her own beverage. He had, after all been a perfect gentleman over dinner, steering conversation to topics that might interest her. And so modest he was in his gentlemanly manner, assuming that he himself might not be one of those interests.

Au contraire.

Because in spite of her conviction that she would not get involved with the man beyond this single, cursory encounter, the more time Winona spent with Mr. Montgomery this evening, the more her interest in him was piqued. And now she was going to seek some answers to the myriad questions circling about her brain. Naturally, though, she would do so in a ladylike fashion.

"Gosh, what's there to tell?" he asked.

"Well, I don't know," she told him. "That's why I'm asking."

He shrugged as he settled his cup back into its saucer. But he focused his gaze intently on her face when he said, "Basically, I'm just a new guy in town who's looking to make a few new…friends. Especially friends of the female persuasion."

Winona eyed him thoughtfully. Well, that was certainly a leading comment, she thought. One that might very well be construed as ungentlemanly. Was he about to err? Was he going to say something suggestive? Would this put an effective end to their time together? And why was she so disappointed to discover that it might?

"Well, you should find no shortage of those," she said carefully. "Friends of the female persuasion, I mean."

"No?" he asked. Politely, she noted, but there was something else in his voice that provoked suspicion. She just couldn't quite say what that something else was. "Do you perchance...have anyone particular in mind?" he asked further.

Winona narrowed her eyes at him. Well, that certainly was a very odd thing to say. He was, after all, having dinner with her, a dinner to which *he* had invited her. Was he hinting that he'd now like for her to introduce him to other women? Was that why he had hoped to make her acquaintance in the first place? Well. That wasn't very gentlemanly at all.

"No," she said cautiously. "I don't have anyone particular in mind. But there are a number of single young women in town, thanks to the university."

"Are there?" he asked, again in that strangely suspicious tone. "And how would you suggest a man go about meeting them? Provided a man wanted to?" he quickly added.

Part of Winona felt crushed that he would ask her such a thing, was surprisingly hurt by the realization that he had invited her to dinner only to use her as an outlet to meet other women. And truly, she couldn't understand why he would think her an appropriate candidate for something like that.

But another part of her—the rational part—reminded her that she shouldn't be at all surprised. Mr. Montgomery was a young, urbane, modern male. It stood to reason that he would seek out women of a similar nature. Clearly he had already seen the folly of asking out a woman such as she. She didn't play the singles game the way one was supposed to play it these days. Obviously, Mr. Montgomery was ready to move on to greener pastures. Still, she had no idea why he would think she might be willing to act as his...shepherdess...while exploring those greener pastures.

Ah, well, she thought, swallowing her disappointment. What had she expected? That he would be a perfect gentleman?

"I'm sorry, Mr. Montgomery," she said softly, avoiding

his gaze, "but you'd do better by yourself, I'm sure. I'm not socially linked to any of the young women in town, save those who work for me. If you're looking for introductions—"

"That's *exactly* what I'm looking for," he said, fairly pouncing on the comment. "Introductions. To women who work for you."

Something cool and heavy settled in Winona's midsection at hearing him spell it out so obviously. "Well, as I said, then," she told him, "you'd be better off on your own."

And as the cool, heavy weight grew heavier and colder still, Winona, having no idea what to say or do next, and wanting very much to escape from what felt like a bad dream, quickly stood. Hastily, she gathered her gloves and bag, which she had placed on the table.

"Good evening, Mr. Montgomery," she said as she turned away. "I thank you very much for dinner. But I only now remembered that I have a previous engagement I absolutely cannot miss. I do apologize for this frightful oversight, but I really must go."

And with those rapidly uttered words, even though she knew it wasn't very polite, Winona went. Quickly.

Five

Winona got as far as the exit before Connor, stunned by her reaction, realized she honestly meant to leave him sitting there all alone. Without thinking, he leaped up, hastily counted out what would pretty much cover dinner and about an 85 percent tip, threw the wad of bills on the table and ran after her.

He'd been so sure that he was being casual and discreet when he'd made his inquiry about introductions, but obviously, he hadn't been subtle at all. Madam Winona must have made him for a cop. She must have realized what he was asking for, where he was trying to lead her, and that was the reason why she was fleeing now—to avoid any further investigation into her illegal activities.

Or else, Conner thought further, she was fleeing because he'd just grossly insulted her, a perfectly nice woman who had no illegal proclivities whatsoever, by inviting her to dinner and asking her to introduce him to other women. This after promising to be a perfect gentleman, too.

Maybe she really did have nothing to do with the prostitution ring working out of her business, he couldn't help pondering further. Maybe she really would be shocked when she discovered what was going on. Maybe he was totally wrong about her. Maybe she really was just a nice, old-fashioned girl. A nice, old-fashioned girl who'd just had her feelings hurt by a mean, twenty-first-century jerk.

Nah, he quickly reassured himself, however halfheartedly. There was little chance that he was wrong about Madam Winona being *Madam* Winona. Connor Monahan's hunches always played out right. Always. His instincts were unimpeachable. And his instincts had told him from the start that there was something fishy about Winona Thornbury, and that she was indeed the woman in charge of the illegal operation working out of her restaurant.

Just because his instincts hadn't been quite so insistent since he'd gotten up close and personal with her, that didn't mean anything. He'd just been swayed by a pretty face and a killer body, that was all. And by a charming smile and a sweet demeanor. And by good manners and demure grace. And by inexplicably erotic little white gloves. Just because his instincts now were howling something totally different from what they had been howling before…

He expelled a growl of restlessness as he followed Winona Thornbury toward the exit. Dammit. He really was beginning to wonder if maybe he was wrong about her. Because the more he found out about her, the less there was that made any sense. Still, there was no evidence to indicate that she *wasn't* involved with the prostitution ring operating out of Winona's. Then again, there was no evidence to indicate that she *was* part of it, either.

Ah, hell. He didn't know what to do. Except go after her now and try to correct the blunder he'd just made. Whatever that blunder was. Whether it be that he'd just jeopardized the investigation—again—or insulted a perfectly nice—and innocent—woman.

"Winona," he called after her as he pushed open the café door and fled into the dark evening. The streetlights had come on during their time in the Garden Path, and now they cast a pale, bluish glow over the storefronts and passersby that lay between him and Winona. She was already half a block ahead of him, but Connor had no trouble finding her among the throngs of people crowding the sidewalk. There just weren't all that many people out tonight who were wearing turn-of-the-century gowns and gloves and marking their steps with a parasol. Go figure.

She didn't turn around when he called her name, though, despite his certainty that she'd heard him. He knew that, because a half-dozen other people *did* turn toward him when he called her name, some even farther down the block than she was herself.

"Winona!" he tried again, a bit louder this time. But still, she ignored him, increasing her speed in her effort to escape.

So he hastened his step, too, pushing his way between more than one group of people, gentlemanly behavior be damned. She had her back to him now. It didn't count. And within moments, Connor was close enough to reach out and cup a hand gently over her shoulder.

"Winona, wait," he said again as he gently spun her around. And the moment he did, every last breath left his lungs in a long, silent *whoosh*.

Good God, he thought when he saw her face. She had tears in her eyes. What the hell…?

"I'm sorry," he told her. Though for the life of him, he had no idea what he was apologizing for. If she *was* a madam, peddling flesh, she didn't deserve an apology. And even if she wasn't, he hadn't said anything all *that* insulting. Had he? Most of the women he knew would have laughed off his request to be introduced around, or else would have given back as good as they got. But none of them, he was certain, would have become teary eyed.

Yet Winona Thornbury had. Man, she was a hard one to figure. How sensitive could a woman be? Then again, maybe she was only crying because she knew Connor was on to her and was about to wreck her operation and throw her keester in jail.

Ah, hell, he thought eloquently again. He didn't know what to think. He only knew that at the moment he felt really, really lousy because he'd made Winona cry.

"I'm sorry," he said again, with more feeling this time—both in his voice and in his intention. He still wasn't sure why he was apologizing, but something told him he'd damned well better. Stranger still was the fact that he sincerely did feel sorry. For what, he had no idea. But he really did regret now what he had said and done.

Winona met his gaze levelly for a moment, silently, the unshed tears coupling with the blue tint of the streetlight to make her eyes appear huge and earnest and brilliant. The tip of her nose was tinted with pink, and her lower lip looked plump and bruised, as if she'd been biting it to keep her emotions in check. And it was with no small effort that Connor somehow prevented himself from dipping his head to hers and covering her mouth with his, in an effort to ease her crushed expression.

She seemed to sense the avenue of his thoughts somehow, because her gaze dropped to his mouth, too, and her lips parted some, as if she weren't quite getting enough air—or maybe because she was thinking about kissing him back. The electric moment passed quickly, however, as she suddenly gave her head a single, swift shake, as if she were trying to clear it of some troubling thought. Then she took a very thoughtful, very deliberate, step in retreat.

"I accept your apology," she said softly. Obviously *she* understood why Connor said he was sorry, even if he was still clueless himself. "Now if you'll excuse me," she added, "I really must be going."

And then she spun around again and began to scurry off

once more. This time, however, Connor was ready for her retreat, and he was right there beside her as she made it.

"I'll walk you to your destination," he said before she had a chance to object. "What kind of man would I be, after all, if I let you go traipsing off into the night all by yourself?"

"I'm scarcely alone, Mr. Montgomery," she told him as she strode resolutely forward, keeping her gaze focused straight ahead. "There are scores of people on the street," she added quickly, tilting her head back in defiance. Or maybe she did that not so much out of defiance as she did because she was trying to keep the tears in her eyes from falling.

Boy, did he feel like a first-class, see-exhibit-A heel.

"Still, it wouldn't be very gentlemanly of me to let you go off without an escort, would it?" he pointed out.

She sniffled a bit—in the most ladylike fashion, to be sure—then told him, in no uncertain terms, "I'm beginning to realize that my initial evaluation of you was correct." And she didn't miss one step as she then turned her head to look him squarely in the eye, adding, "You are no gentleman, sir."

And as if that weren't enough to send something chilly and awful blustering through what would have passed for a heart in any other man, one single, fat tear tumbled down her cheek as she made her pronouncement. And seeing it, Connor felt a frosty lash of self-loathing thrash his belly.

Instead of disagreeing with her—how could he?—he only turned his attention forward, shoved his hands deep into his pockets and kept walking alongside her. "You found me out," he concurred. "I guess you can't make a silk purse out of a sow's ear after all, can you?"

"Well, I wouldn't say that," she countered softly. She, too, turned to look ahead once more, her pace still clipped, but slowing a bit now. "I just don't think you *want* to be a silk purse, that's all."

"And you think I should aspire to that?" he asked. "I mean, what's so great about being a silk purse? They're small and flimsy—there's nothing to them. And they have strings attached."

"Indeed they do," she agreed, sounding sad again. "And you, I'm certain, would never go for having strings attached. Nor are you small or flimsy or insubstantial."

"Then why do you think I should be a silk purse?" he asked.

"I never said you should be one," she told him. "Frankly, Mr. Montgomery, I can't see you being happy as a silk purse."

"But I'm right at home as a sow's ear, is that what you're saying?" he asked dryly.

"No," she readily conceded again. "You're not that, either. You're somewhere in between, I should think. I'm not sure what you are exactly."

"Well, that makes two of us," he told her. "Because you sure are a mystery to me, too, lady."

She stopped walking then, so Connor did, too, turning to face her fully. She eyed him cryptically, but the tears were gone from her eyes now, her nose was no longer pink, and the bruising of her mouth had been replaced by the fullness and ripeness and lusciousness that he remembered. Nevertheless, he still wanted to kiss her. Wanted to kiss her and touch her and peel that chaste white dress from her ivory skin, then taste every last naked inch of her before burying himself as deeply inside her as he could, while she murmured his name into the darkness, again and again and again....

"Do you really have someplace else you need to be?" he asked her, the explicit image still raging in his brain. "Or was that just your polite way of dumping me?"

The merest hint of a smile curled the corners of her lips. "I suppose my appointment isn't all *that* urgent," she replied.

"It's a nice night," he remarked. "And it's still young. You said so yourself not long ago."

She dipped her head forward in acknowledgment, and the primness of the gesture only accelerated Connor's desire to...know her better. "I suppose I did," she said.

"We could take a walk through the neighborhood," he suggested.

"So that you might use the opportunity to make the acquaintance of a few young ladies?" she asked.

He shook his head and said, "No. So I can make the acquaintance of one young lady in particular. The one I'm with right now."

"I'm not particularly young, Mr. Montgomery," she reminded him matter-of-factly.

He smiled. "Gee, I didn't think ladies ever divulged their ages."

"I'd think that would be up to the individual lady to decide. As for me, I just think the years that separate us would be something you'd be wise to remember."

He eyed her thoughtfully. "Why?"

"Because there is more than a decade between us," she said.

He shook his head. "No there's not. I just turned twenty-nine. You're not quite ten year older than me."

"I wasn't speaking in chronological terms."

His eyebrows shot up in surprise. "Then what...?"

But Connor never finished his question, and Winona never answered it. She only smiled sweetly and held up her hand, silently indicating that she was ready to take his arm. Her forwardness surprised him, but he was happy to oblige, and deftly held up his arm. When she curled her fingers lightly over the fabric of his jacket, he noticed she had donned her gloves again, and something inside him tightened dangerously.

Those gloves. God. She'd taken them off once they arrived at the restaurant, and he hadn't been able to take his eyes off of her as she'd done so. Hell, he'd watched women remove their underwear with less passion than he'd felt as Winona had slowly, slowly, oh, so slowly unbuttoned those gloves and drawn them down over her wrists, her hands, her fingers. By the time she'd placed them gently on the table beside her little silk purse, he'd felt the stirrings of a hard-on and had thanked his lucky stars that the table between them had concealed his condition.

It made no sense. Here was a woman wrapped up tighter and more thoroughly than any normal human being had a need to be wrapped, and Connor was more turned on than he'd ever been in his life. Certainly he was more turned on than he'd ever been by a woman wearing far, far less. And he was beginning to suspect that his arousal had nothing to do with the fact that Winona might very well be a mistress of pleasure, who knew how to…do things to him that would never occur to other women—or else would thoroughly repulse other women.

No, Connor was becoming more than a little worried that his preoccupation with the delicious Winona was the result of something far more insidious that simple lust. Because he very much feared that he was beginning to—gulp—like her.

God almighty, he thought as they strode forward. Could it possibly get any worse?

Winona never, ever, under any circumstances, stayed out later than 11:00 p.m. It was, of course, helpful that in keeping with this rule she lived in the same building where she worked. But even had that not been the case, she simply wasn't the type of person to keep late hours outside those required for her job. She supposed that when all was said and done, restaurateur wasn't, exactly, the prime occupation for a woman of her bent, but it was what she loved, and it was what she did best, and since it did require keeping late hours in order to accommodate one's clientele, she had no objection to the late evenings, professionally speaking.

Socially, however, Winona was no night owl. Probably because, socially, she was, well, inert. Which made it doubly surprising when she and Mr. Montgomery returned to her home at just past two o'clock in the morning. She was amazed at how quickly the hours had passed and at how they had managed to fill those hours with animated conversation and spirited entertainment.

After leaving the café—and after that unfortunate exchange that Winona had decided to put down to misunderstanding and forget all about—they had forged a kind of companionship that had been surprisingly pleasant. They had stopped for ice cream at one point, and enjoyed it while seated at a small, outdoor table, watching the people pass by and indulging in agreeable conversation. Then they had stumbled upon, and been just in time for, a showing of Jean Renoir's *Beauty and the Beast*—in French with subtitles, no less—at a local art house. And there had been something so wonderfully intimate about sharing popcorn and lemonade with Mr. Montgomery in the darkened theater. She had no idea why. But it had been fun. Quite fun. Astonishingly fun.

They'd spent the remainder of the evening strolling through the streets of Bloomington, mingling with the college crowd where Winona had always felt so strangely at home, in spite of her propensity for another age and other customs. All in all, the night had been, well, lovely. To say the least. And all in all, Mr. Montgomery had been, well, charming. To say the least.

Now as they strolled through the gate that led into her garden, Winona realized that she had no idea what to do or say. The restaurant was closed, and her employees were gone for the night, so she and Mr. Montgomery were very much alone. Laurel had left the usual lights burning, but the sign was off, and the place was very clearly locked up tight. The antique porch light hanging over her front/side door was lit, but the twenty-five-watt bulb threw out only the merest puddle of light.

She halted just inside the gate and was about to turn to Mr. Montgomery, to tell him she was fine and could see herself in, but he stopped her by taking her elbow lightly and saying, very softly, "I'll see you to the door."

It was the very softly part that prevented her from objecting. Something in his voice was just…irresistible. So she only nodded silently and allowed him to lead her toward the door, then became inordinately interested in fishing her key out of her bag. But somehow the key kept eluding her, and she never could quite grasp it enough to withdraw it. By the time they reached her door, she was still fumbling for it. She heard Mr. Montgomery chuckle, but not in any way other than that he was mildly amused. So she let a few chuckles of her own escape, and somehow that eased the knot of tension that had threatened to tie the moment.

"It's the gloves," he told her as he reached for her bag. Effortlessly he located her keys, holding them up in one hand as if they were a trophy, giving them a triumphant little jingle as he smiled. Then he gestured her aside to unlock and open her front door, dropped the keys back into her bag and handed it back to her.

"Thank you. I'm usually not such a fumble-fingers, regardless of the situation," she told him. "It has nothing to do with the gloves, I assure you."

His smile grew broader, and as she gazed at him, Winona noted how the yellow glow of the porch light ignited amber fires in his hair, and how it made his blue eyes seem to glow silver somehow.

"Then it must be something else that's got you feeling nervous," he said quietly.

"I-I-I'm not nervous," she denied nervously.

"Aren't you?" he asked with much too much confidence.

She shook her head slowly but knew she wasn't being at all truthful. "Certainly not," she insisted anyway. "Why would I be nervous?"

He studied her in silence for a moment, then, "Maybe because you know how much I want to kiss you good night," he said quietly.

A runnel of heat splashed through her midsection at hearing his remark. "Do you?" she asked.

He nodded, his gaze never leaving hers. "I do."

"I...I see."

"So...may I?"

"K-k-k-kiss me?" she faltered.

He nodded again, still focused intently on her face, her eyes, her mouth. "I promise I'll be a gentleman."

"I...ah...well...you see...I mean...um...that is..." Winona swallowed hard and willed herself to be firm with him. Then she heard herself say, quite firmly, "All right."

Evidently, it took a moment for her consent to register with him, because for a moment Mr. Montgomery only gazed down at her face as if he were still awaiting her reply. Then her response must have finally dawned on him, because his handsome features went lax, his silver-blue eyes darkened to the depth and texture of storm clouds, and his lips parted the merest bit. Then he took a small step forward, bent his head to hers and brushed his lips lightly over her own, once...twice...three times, before finally pulling back.

The entire exchange lasted only seconds, and his body never touched hers save the scant, sweet seduction of his mouth on her own. Really, his kiss had been almost chaste. Yet somehow, Winona suddenly felt as if she were on fire. He might as well have just run his hands over every inch of her naked body, caressing, carousing, exploring, entering. Only when she opened her eyes did she realize she had closed them. And only then did she see that Mr. Montgomery had been as turbulently affected by the encounter as she.

And then she heard herself say the strangest thing. "Would you like to come in for a cup of tea, Mr. Montgomery?"

And he surprised her even more by replying, "No, thank you, Miss Thornbury. Perhaps another time." Then he quietly bade her good-night, dipped his head in farewell and turned to walk away. Only once did he look back, after closing the gate behind him. He lifted a hand in fond farewell, softly bade her good-night one final time and made his way down the dark street, toward the spot at the end of the block where he had parked his car.

And as she watched him go, Winona realized she had no idea whether what had just happened between the two of them was a good thing or not.

Connor drove straight back to his place after leaving Winona Thornbury's house. *His place* in this regard being *not* the Budget Motor Lodge, Bloomington, where he'd made his home for the past few weeks, but his real home—Marigold, Indiana. It was nearly 3:00 a.m. when he arrived at his apartment, but he didn't care. The last thing he felt like doing was sleeping. No, he was fairly sure that, thanks to his reaction to the little kiss he'd planted on Winona less than an hour ago, he'd never be sleeping again.

And that, of course, would be due to the fact that he was currently suffering from a state of consummate arousal heretofore unknown in the annals of sexual history. At least, that was probably how Winona Thornbury would have described his condition—had she not been too nice and old-fashioned to describe something like that. At least, she *acted* much too nice and old-fashioned to describe something like that. The jury was still out on whether or not she was, in fact, a nice, old-fashioned girl. At any rate, to Connor, his current predicament was more appropriately described as a simple raging hard-on that wouldn't go away. Even though he'd had almost an hour of boring driving to calm himself down. There would be no calming down for some time from this.

And that, of course, would be due to the fact that he had spent that boring almost-hour of driving thinking about Winona Thornbury and about the concussion of heat that had bolted through him with the first soft brush of his mouth over hers. It had been a punch of desire that had only doubled and then tripled with that second and third caress.

Just what the hell had gotten into him? he wondered as he let himself into his dark, silent apartment. His *too* dark, *too* silent apartment. Immediately he began prowling restlessly around the living room, turning on lights and the CD player and the TV and the radio, because he needed *something* to distract him, dammit, and take his mind off Winona. But even with everything blaring and shining at him, Connor still felt the subtle, quiet tug of Winona. Instead of his Spartanly furnished, Swedishly influenced bachelor's apartment, he saw himself, in his mind's eye, surrounded by the bounty and beauty of her house—herself—instead.

Why did she have him so tied up in knots? he wondered again. Was it some kind of game on her part? Had he been right about her all along? Was she a madam or a hooker or both, simply trying to hold on to the only business she knew, the only way she knew how? *Did* she know he was a cop? *Was* she trying to throw him off the trail? Because he couldn't think of any reason why a woman like her would be able to arouse such a rawly sexual response in him, unless it was because she knew some age-old, rawly sexual secret for seizing a man's libido the way she had his, and sending it through the wringer—the way she had his.

She had to be a madam or a hooker or both, Connor told himself. She had to be. It was the only explanation that made any sense. And she had to be working some kind of madam/hooker mojo on him to make him feel the way he was feeling now. He was burning up inside. He'd started burning the minute he began watching her taking off those little white gloves of hers, and he'd been on fire all night long. And that kiss...

Holy Mary, Mother of God. That kiss. He'd barely touched her mouth with his, but the minute he'd made contact, every desire, every need, every hunger he possessed had roared up inside him demanding to be sated. Had he taken her up on her invitation to come inside for tea—yeah, right—he was more than confident that, at this very moment, he and the luscious Winona would be tangled up in sweaty sheets, doing things with each other, doing things *to* each other, that he probably wouldn't recover from for days.

So why the hell hadn't he taken her up on her offer? he asked himself for perhaps the hundredth time since driving away from her place. Why wasn't he in her house right now, amid all that frilly, feminine stuff, showing her what a man could do?

Probably, he thought, because it would have compromised the investigation even worse than he had already compromised it. Especially if she *had* made him as a cop.

Ah, dammit, why couldn't he figure this thing out? he wondered as he freed his necktie from its loosened knot and tugged it rabidly from his collar. Why was it that the more he thought about it, the more confused he became, and the less sense all of it made?

The evidence was there, he reminded himself. They knew—they *knew*—there was a call-girl ring operating out of Winona's. All they had left to do was find out the particulars, and who was heading it up. The logical conclusion was that Winona herself was running it. But something inside Connor, something that was entirely new to him, told him otherwise.

He should have accepted her offer, he told himself. He should have gone into her house under the pretense of having tea and seen where she would lead him. If she had invited him into her bed, he would have known once and for all that she wasn't the nice, old-fashioned girl she pretended to be. Not that that would give him any more evidence that she was running an illegal operation, but it damned sure would have cleared up any confusion he might have about her as a law-abiding, morally upstanding human being.

Not that everybody who slept with their companion on the first date was doing anything illegal, Connor quickly reminded himself. If that were the rule, then he himself would be doing time for more than one offense. He wasn't even the kind of man who thought it was a matter of loose morals to jump right into bed with someone. Why should it be immoral to satisfy what was a natural, God-given urge?

He did, however, take exception to someone who pretended to be something he or she was not. He disregarded, for now, the fact that he himself was currently guilty of misrepresenting himself—he had a good reason, dammit. And had he been making Winona's sheets sweaty and tangled at that moment, he would have known that her prim, chaste, old-fashioned act was precisely that—an act.

Which still didn't provide him with anything about Winona Thornbury that he hadn't already known about her before tonight. Except, of course, that her mouth was every bit as soft and sweet and succulent as he had dreamed it would be.

He groaned with much feeling and made his way to his bedroom, switching on more lights, turning on more music in his wake. But all he saw then was another sparsely furnished room with lots of blond wood and stark designs that somehow seemed artificial to him. Odd, that he'd always liked the clean, uncluttered lines of his life before. And the rampant music assaulting his ears, music he had very much enjoyed previously, suddenly sounded disjointed and discordant now.

Shoving the troubling thought aside, Connor jerked off his jacket and tossed it onto a chair, then went to work on the buttons of his shirt. And all the while, he tried not to think about what it might have been like for Winona to be doing the honors instead.

She would have taken her time, he was certain, unbuttoning his shirt with all the unhurried patience she had shown for her gloves. Then she would have skimmed the garment slowly from his shoulders and dragged her fingertips leisurely down his chest, curling her fingers in the dark hair scattered there. Then she would have pushed her hands lower still, raking her fingers down over his rib cage and flat belly, to the waistband of his trousers, where she would free the button and zipper, and tuck her hand inside. And then she would cup her fingers lovingly, possessively over his—

Connor groaned again, with even more feeling this time, reaching down to unfasten his trousers himself, because they were becoming much, *much* too tight for his comfort. Then he left his bedroom to head for the bathroom instead. No way was he ready to go to bed yet. Not alone, at any rate. But a nice, cold shower seemed like a very good idea. And the more alone he was for that, the better. Because somehow he suspected that Winona Thornbury could turn even an iceberg into a steam bath, just like that.

And God almighty, he had no idea what to do.

Six

Winona didn't see Connor Montgomery in her restaurant the night following their, ah…little interlude, and she wasn't sure whether she should be delighted or upset about the development. Nor did she see him Wednesday night— and she had the same uncertain reaction then. He didn't come in Thursday, either. Nor did he make an appearance on Friday. Nor Saturday. And on all of those days that he wasn't there, Winona experienced a whirlwind of conflicting reactions. She was by turns relieved and worried, gratified and disappointed. Not once, however, did she feel content.

By Sunday morning she was beginning to wonder if perhaps she had simply imagined Connor Montgomery into existence, because he seemed to have vanished completely from the face of the Earth. She could find no evidence of him anywhere. Well, nowhere other than her fantasies, delusions and dreams, she was forced to confess. And in *those,* he most definitely had a life of his own.

Her dreams at night, especially, had been filled with him. During the day, whenever she caught herself thinking about Connor Montgomery, she was usually able to distract herself with thoughts of something else, or by keeping busy in the restaurant. But in sleep she had no such luxury. In sleep she was helpless to restrain her thoughts of him, and in sleep her thoughts of him were nothing short of tempestuous.

Even now, fully awake, as she sat in her office trying to clear up some paperwork she should have completed days ago, Winona couldn't quite keep memories of him at bay. Or, more accurately, she couldn't quite keep memories of her dreams of him at bay. Because those dreams, the ones that had come to her every single night, had been outrageous, ignominious, licentious, *scandalous.*

Well, all right, perhaps not ignominious, Winona conceded reluctantly. She certainly hadn't felt disgraced by any of her dreams. Not really. But she had most certainly been scandalized by them. Never in her life, *never,* had she entertained the kind of graphic mental imagery that her dreams of Connor Montgomery brought with them. Even when she had enjoyed her brief, ah…odyssey of sexual discovery…with Stanley Wadsworth, Winona hadn't come close to experiencing the sort of reactions she had experienced when she had been with Connor in a completely fantastical way.

Because she awoke from such dreams in quite a state, panting for breath, her heart raging wildly, her nightgown bunched about her hips, her sheets tangled between her legs, her body hot and dewy from the dampness of her perspiration and her own release. Never had she felt with a very corporeal Stanley the sort of things she felt with an illusory Connor. She had even ceased to think of him as Mr. Montgomery, which was thoroughly unlike her. But how could she use such a formality with the man when she had experienced such a...such a...such a *fulfillment* with him, if only in her dreams?

And what on earth was she going to say to him the next time she saw him?

Perhaps she *wouldn't* see him again, she told herself as she placed another sealed envelope atop the stack that had collected since morning. Perhaps, after spending such a moderate, unsophisticated evening with her, he had decided he wasn't interested in her after all. His kiss good-night had held anything but passion—for him, at any rate, even if that hadn't been the case with her at all.

And he had declined her invitation to come in for tea—though, truly, she still couldn't imagine now what had come over her to issue such an invitation in the first place. Not only had it *not* been teatime, but Winona was certain it was imprudent for her to suggest that she would have enjoyed his company in the wee hours of the morning. Because there was a very specific activity that men and women traditionally enjoyed at such an hour. And it most certainly *wasn't* tea. Why should she encourage Connor to think that she might have been interested in indulging in such an activity with him?

Unless, of course, it was because she very much wanted to indulge in such an activity with him.

Oh, dear, Winona thought. There she went again, thinking illicit thoughts about Connor in the light of day. Not only was that *not* conducive to good work habits, it *was* conducive to madness. Because it would only lead to frustration. Frustration and...other things she had no business inviting into her life.

But her worry over the whole situation was probably pointless anyway. He hadn't kissed her passionately. He hadn't accepted her invitation to...whatever. In fact, Connor seemed like the kind of man who would go for women of a much faster lifestyle than Winona practiced herself.

Which made her wonder again why he had asked her to go out with him in the first place.

She sighed heavily and stood, gathering up the assortment of mail on her desk. She had dressed that morning for work in a calf-length dress of pale-rose cotton. It was an unusually plain dress for her, in that the only decoration came in the dozens of pearl buttons marching down the front, the white lace trim on the three-quarter-length sleeves and a white lace collar that she had pinned at the throat with an antique cameo. But work was the last thing on Winona's mind today. Sundays were generally slow and leisurely at the restaurant, a limited brunch and an afternoon tea—a real tea, not the *whatever* kind of tea to which she had invited Connor last weekend—followed by an early closing before dinner, so that she could enjoy *some*thing resembling a weekend.

Perhaps no one would notice if she slipped out for a bit, she thought, gazing at the handful of mail. A short stroll to the post office up the street would do her good. It would be closed, of course, but she could drop the mail into the mailbox and have one less thing to do tomorrow. Right now, she felt restless, edgy and the day outside was lovely—clear and cool, with the mingling scents of apples and drying leaves vying for possession of the breeze. The fresh air, she was certain, would do her good and might invigorate her with a new sense of purpose.

Oh, yes. A new purpose. She definitely needed one of those.

After checking to make sure everything was running smoothly, and after alerting her host to her destination, Winona donned her gloves and draped an embroidered shawl fashioned of creamy white silk over her shoulders. Then she gathered up her mail and headed out into the street. She was halfway down the block when she noticed a familiar figure in a dark suit striding toward her. Her breath caught at the sight of him, her heart skipped an already erratic beat and she stumbled over an irregular brick in the sidewalk.

Connor Montgomery had returned to Bloomington. And, as was his habit, he was coming right at her.

Holy moly, Connor thought when he saw Winona striding oh, so casually up the street in his direction. To put it in much more polite—and much less panicky—terms than he was feeling at the moment. He hadn't meant to run into her just yet. He still had a whole speech to rehearse before he would be ready to see her again. He wasn't even sure he'd worked up the nerve to walk back into her life yet. Hell, he wasn't even sure he was ready to walk back into her restaurant yet. Even after a week of mulling things over, he still had no idea what he intended to do.

He had spent the bulk of the previous week holed up in Marigold, going over—yet again—every scrap of evidence he had in his possession regarding the Winona Thornbury case. He had called the Bloomington boys on a number of occasions to compare notes with them, had followed up on things he hadn't been sure about the first time, had, for the most part, reinvestigated the entire investigation.

His conclusion? Oh, that was an easy one. He was more confused now than ever.

Where before he had been absolutely convinced that Winona was not only involved in the operation working out of her restaurant, but spearheading it, after the evening the two of them had spent together, Connor had begun to have his doubts. Because instead of being an unctuous, opportunistic madam bent on making an illegal buck off the backs of young women, Winona really did seem like nothing more than a nice, old-fashioned girl who ran a successful restaurant for a living.

She hadn't seemed to have any hidden agenda, illicit or otherwise. She hadn't seemed to have anything to hide at all. Certainly she didn't seem to have as much to hide as

Connor did himself. So who was really the liar misrepresenting themself in this relationship, hmm?

Best not to think about that one for now.

There *was* one thing he *had* figured out, however. He had figured out *why* he had begun to question his conviction that Winona was running an illegal operation. It was very simple, really. He shouldn't have been surprised by the discovery at all. But once he'd made the discovery, he'd been astonished.

He'd begun to question his conviction about her because, to put it in incredibly simple terms, he didn't *want* Winona to be spearheading an illegal operation. And the reason he didn't want her to be spearheading an illegal operation was because he *did* want *her*. Badly. And now he was afraid his attraction to her was going to color his opinion of her, maybe even blindside him completely. And if that happened, it would only jeopardize his ability to complete this investigation to its fullest extent.

Oh, right, Monahan, like you haven't jeopardized this investigation in a million other ways already.

The voice—not to mention the sentiment—was a familiar one, because Connor had been hearing both all week. Part of him was still confident that he hadn't done anything wrong where the investigation was concerned, that he hadn't crossed any lines yet, even if he'd maybe blurred a few. That part of him was sure that every action he had completed *would* hold up in court. Pretty much. With a good DA prosecuting. And a lot of luck.

But another part of Connor feared that maybe, just maybe, he was going about this thing the wrong way. And that maybe, just maybe, he'd done one or two things that were going to get him hammered. Hard.

Worse than that, though, was the fact that, the closer he got to Winona, the blurrier those aforementioned uncrossed lines became. And the blurrier those lines became, the easier they were going to be to cross. And once they were crossed… Well. Once they were crossed, there would be no going back over them. Connor just wasn't sure yet what would be considered crossing them and what would be considered blurring them a little more.

Probably, he thought as he watched Winona approach, her luscious body moving with all the grace and rhythm of a well-oiled machine, engaging in wild monkey lovin' with a suspect in a criminal case would be one of those once-crossed-never-comin'-back-over-the-line things.

Dammit.

And that, he knew, was what had really kept him in Marigold all week. He'd been reasonably certain Monday night—or, rather, early Tuesday morning—that if he didn't put some distance, both geographic and temporal, between himself and Winona, then he was most definitely going to cross that line. Because thoughts of Winona had just naturally overlapped with thoughts of wild monkey lovin' in Connor's mind. Day and night. Night and day. All. Week. Long. There was no two ways about that.

And now that he saw her striding toward him down the street, as he watched the subtle sway of her full hips and the way her pink dress swished about her well-turned calves, as he registered the little white gloves that he found so profoundly arousing, as he noted the long line of buttons down the front of her dress and wondered what it would be like to loose them one by one…

Connor sighed heavily and began to think that he hadn't put nearly enough time and distance between them. Maybe if he went to the planet Pluto for a couple of millennia, that might take care of it….

But instead of turning tail to hide himself to the nearest NASA facility, Connor continued to walk forward. He simply could not help himself. It was as if Winona had a string twined around her little finger whose other end was attached soundly to his libido. And she just kept coiling that string around her finger, little by little by little, pulling him closer and closer and closer, until he had no chance of escape.

And then, suddenly, she was tripping over something in the cobbled walk, and her stride became more hurried and less certain, and the next thing Connor knew, she was stumbling forward with real speed, grasping for something to hold on to that didn't exist and losing her footing and going down, and he was running forward to catch her, and just in the nick of time, he did.

Boy, did he catch her.

Because by the time all was said and done—or, at least, by the time all was done, since neither of them said a word, save Winona's softly uttered "Oops"—he was holding her in his arms, one roped protectively around her waist, the other across her back. And then he was pulling her entire body closer to his own, ostensibly to steady her, but actually because he really, really, really wanted to know what it would be like to have her that close. And because he'd really, really missed her this week.

Nice, he realized quickly. It felt really, really nice to have her close.

The soft aroma of lavender enveloped him as he drew Winona nearer, nearly intoxicating him with its sweet scent. Or maybe it was Winona herself who intoxicated him. All Connor knew was that he had his arms full of soft, warm, fragrant woman, a woman whose absence he had felt keenly all week long. And as that knowledge settled over him, he reacted the only way he knew how. He bent his head to hers and kissed her.

Not, however, the way his instincts were commanding him to kiss her at the moment—by opening his mouth over hers and consuming her in one big, greedy bite while he rushed his hands all over her body, unfastening her clothing as he went so that he could investigate all the soft parts he wanted to investigate. Somehow, in that moment, Connor knew—he just *knew*—there was going to be time for all that in the future. In the not-so-distant future, too. So, for now, he forced himself to be satisfied with another one of those innocent, chaste little kisses like he'd given her the other night. One that told her merely, "Oh, hey, it's good to see ya again."

Even at that, though, he was surprised when Winona did nothing to stop him. On the contrary, when Connor made himself pull away from her, when he lifted his head from hers to gaze down at her face, she only curled her gloved fingers more insistently into the lapels of his jacket, as if she had every intention of pulling him back down for more. For a moment her eyes remained closed, her lips slightly pursed, as if, in her mind, at least, she was still kissing him. Then, little by little, her eyes fluttered open, looking dreamy and uncertain and…and…and…

Connor caught his breath at the realization—and *not a little turned-on.*

So Winona Thornbury wasn't quite so nice and old-fashioned as she seemed, he thought. She wasn't quite as chaste and innocent as he'd begun to think she was. Because clearly there were fires burning behind that buttoned-up, battened-down facade. All he had to do now was figure out a way to…stoke them.

Later, he reminded himself. But *not* too much later…

Her eyes were even bluer than he remembered, he noted as he drank his visual fill of her, and her mouth seemed fuller, riper, more delicious. Her cheeks were stained with the merest hint of pink, though whether that was a result of the cool breeze circling them or something else entirely, he couldn't have said.

For one long moment the two of them gazed into each others' eyes, Connor with his arms still looped around Winona's back, she with her fingers still curled into the fabric of his jacket.

And then, suddenly, very, very softly, she said, "Why, Mr. Montgomery. How nice to see you again."

Connor smiled. Oh, she was so transparent. "It's good to see you, too, Miss Thornbury. You're looking well." *And you don't feel too bad, either,* he added to himself. Hoo-boy, was that an understatement.

Still focusing on his eyes, still speaking in that fanciful little voice, still held tenderly in his arms, she replied, "Thank you."

And still holding her tenderly, Connor responded quietly, "You're welcome."

For another moment she only gazed at him in silence, clearly still not realizing what a compromising position she was in. "I was beginning to think you might have moved away," she told him. "You were gone for so long."

"Ah...business trip," he said off the top of his head. "I, um, I had to be away for a business trip last week."

"I see," she said. Still dreamily. Still gazing into his eyes. Still holding firmly to his jacket. "You didn't mention that on Monday."

Connor nodded slowly. "Ah, yeah. Well. You see. About that. It was, um, sudden. Really sudden. I didn't have time to do much more than throw a couple of things into a suitcase and head out."

Boy, was that a lie, he thought. Not only had his trip had nothing to do with business, but he hadn't even taken time to pack. Just how much longer would it be before he could tell Winona Thornbury something—anything—that was the truth?

"Oh, my," she said, sounding a little breathless now. "I do hope everything is all right."

"It's great," Connor told her, smiling genuinely now because at last he could speak the truth. "Everything is just fine."

More than fine, he thought. In that moment, at least, everything was perfect. Because he was standing outside on a spectacular Sunday afternoon, beneath an endless blue sky and a canopy of trees kissed with scarlet and amber and gold. And he was holding Winona Thornbury in his arms and gazing at her in her pink dress and antique pin, with her blond hair escaping from the terse bun she had pinned at the back of her head, a few errant strands of gold being blown about her face by a soft autumn breeze. And what a face. Eyes that put the color and clarity of the sky to shame, cheeks as soft and ivory as porcelain and lips as dewy and red as roses after rain.

And Holy Mary, Mother of God, Connor had turned into a poet, and didn't even know it.

With much reluctance he steadied her on her feet and released her, cupping his hands over her upper arms until she seemed able to right herself. It took a moment for her to realize what was going on, to recognize how the two of them had passed the last few minutes, because she didn't release Connor right away, nor did she ever remove her gaze from his face. When she finally *did* seem to understand how she had just spent the last tiny bit of her life— being embraced by a man in the middle of the street on a leisurely Sunday afternoon—she *did* glance away from him. Very hastily. Very uncomfortably. Then she blushed furiously and bent to pick up some letters Connor just now realized she had been carrying and had dropped at some point during their embrace.

"Well," she said as she straightened, sorting through her mail as if she wanted very desperately to remind herself where each and every piece of correspondence was headed. "Well, well," she reiterated as she went through the letters a second time. And then, as she sifted through them a third time, she added, "Well...well...well."

"Well," Connor concurred, grinning. She was awfully cute when she was off-kilter. And if she got this nervous after a simple hello kiss, he couldn't wait to see what she would be like when she lost herself completely to her own passion.

Because in that moment, he became absolutely certain

that he would see her lose herself completely to her own passion. Better yet, he'd see her lose herself completely to his passion, too. And he to hers. And that was going to be even more enjoyable.

"Well," she said one last time. She finally lifted her gaze to his, then immediately shot it away once more. "It was, ah…it was nice seeing you again, Mr. Montgomery," she told him. She turned her attention then to a nonexistent smudge she seemed intent on erasing from her left glove. "I'm glad you made it back from your trip safely and soundly. Now, if you'll excuse me, I—"

"Have lunch with me."

Connor wasn't sure what had made him issue the invitation—or voice the edict, whatever—seeing as how he still had no idea what to say to her after giving her not one, but now two, kisses. He still wasn't sure how he felt, still wasn't convinced he hadn't compromised the investigation of Winona's restaurant, still wasn't certain he was doing the right thing. Hell, he wasn't even certain what thing he was doing.

But, somehow he just couldn't tolerate the thought of her walking past him, alone, and going about her life without him. It didn't seem natural for some reason. It didn't seem right. He wanted to be with her. In whatever way he could. And if that meant compromising the investigation, then… then…then…

Then he just wouldn't think about that right now.

Winona glanced back up at him quickly when he issued his invitation—or voiced his edict, whatever—and although she didn't look away this time, he could see she wasn't any too comfortable meeting his gaze.

"I'm sorry? What did you say?" she asked.

"I said, 'Have lunch with me,'" he repeated.

"But I…I…I…"

"At Winona's," he further prodded. "My treat."

She studied him for a moment in silence, her lips slightly

parted, as if there was something on the tip of her tongue that she needed to say. Naturally, Connor's instinct was to lean in again and press his own open mouth to hers, but he decided to wait until later. A little later, anyway. When they weren't standing out in the middle of Bloomington, for all the world to see. But not too much later, because, as always, after spending only a few moments in Winona's presence, he was burning up inside. And he suspected he was going to keep on burning—and Winona would, too—until the two of them did something to douse those fires.

"But I…I have to mail these," she said, holding her correspondence up for his inspection.

With a smile Connor plucked them easily out of her hand and strode exactly five paces back whence he had come, where a mailbox stood stoically at the edge of the walk. He pulled the metal door open with a soft *creeeeak,* dropped the letters inside, and closed it again with a muffled *clonk.* Then he recovered the five paces to stand before Winona and smiled some more.

"There," he told her. "All mailed. Now it's lunchtime."

"But I…I have to get back to work," she said.

"You close in less than two hours, don't you?"

She nodded.

He grinned some more. "I'll wait."

"But two hours—"

"Is nothing," he assured her. "Not when I think about how long I've been waiting for you already."

She narrowed her eyes some at his cryptic comment, and Connor hoped like hell she didn't ask him to elaborate on it. Not because he didn't want to have to lie to her again about the investigation. And not because he didn't want to lie to her about anything else, either.

But because he honestly didn't understand any better than she did why he'd said it at all.

Seven

By the time Winona closed her restaurant and locked up behind all of her employees, she was a nervous wreck. Because by then, Connor Montgomery had been sitting in the otherwise deserted bar area of the restaurant, sipping coffee and reading the Sunday paper—and watching her *very* intently every time she entered the dining area—for nearly two hours. And at the end of those two hours, thanks to the barrage of incendiary looks he had blasted her way, every nerve ending Winona possessed was *on fire*.

Well, thanks to those incendiary looks, *and* the fact that she kept replaying in her mind, over and over and over again, that lovely little kiss he had given her when she'd stumbled, quite literally, into his arms earlier that afternoon.

Yes, indeed, memories of that embrace had gone a *looong* way toward stoking the fires he'd set a week ago. Because memories of that kiss had inevitably reminded Winona—over and over and *over* again—of the other kiss she'd enjoyed with Connor the last time they had been together. And recollections of both had only doubled what had already become a strange, and almost intolerable, need for him.

She still couldn't imagine what had come over her to allow him such a flagrant liberty this afternoon, kissing her right out there in the great wide open. It was shocking enough that she had succumbed to him so readily last weekend, but at least then, his kiss had come about through a reasonable set of circumstances. The two of them had been out on a prearranged date, and traditionally, a kiss goodnight wasn't outside the realm of possibility at the conclusion of such an interlude.

Many women allowed their escorts a kiss good-night during such a state of affairs, Winona reminded herself. Though, indeed, perhaps *affairs* wasn't the best word to use in this situation. She hastily shook the thought off. No matter. From what she understood, many women even allowed greater liberties than just a kiss at the climax of a first date. Though, perhaps *climax* wasn't such a good word to use, either, she thought further, feeling flushed for some reason. Honestly, she had no idea why she was having so much trouble with semantics today.

At any rate, this afternoon, there had been no excuse for her outrageous behavior with Connor. Why, before she'd even had the chance to properly greet him, she'd been kissing him. And what kind of woman kissed a man before she even said, Hello, how are you, so lovely to see you again? Worse, she couldn't imagine what had come over her to enjoy such a scandalous kiss *so much.*

Never in her life had Winona experienced the feelings that Connor made her feel. Never had she known such feelings even existed for a person to experience. She had thought the height of her sexual discovery had come in the arms of her ex-fiancé, Stanley Wadsworth. But her brief time with Stanley had done nothing to prepare her for this…this…this explosion of sensation that erupted inside her merely by having Connor come near her. And if this was the way she felt after a few innocent kisses from him and a thoroughly benign embrace, what would it be like to completely give herself over to—

No, she assured herself. That wasn't going to happen. She would not succumb to the desires and needs that Connor incited in her. She would not. She wasn't going to give herself over to a man again without the benefit of matrimony to cement that giving. And Connor Montgomery was clearly *not* the marrying kind.

Still, she thought, it might be rather interesting to see what would occur if—

No, she told herself more firmly this time. It wasn't going to happen. Not until she had a firm commitment in the form of a wedding ring and church service. Period.

But maybe just once, she backpedaled. Just to see if he was really as—

NO! she proclaimed to herself more adamantly. She would not succumb. She wouldn't. She would *not.*

Winona repeated the vow again and again in her brain as she strode toward the bar to find him, as if in doing so, the words might generate some magical incantation that would ward off evil. Then she saw Connor seated where he had been seated all afternoon, gazing at her with that wicked, wicked smile, his blue eyes blazing with intent as he watched her stride toward him.

And she realized there was nothing in the world that would ward him off, once he set his mind to…whatever he'd set it to. All Winona could do was hope he had more willpower than she had herself. Because she very much suspected in that moment that, should Connor decided he wanted her—really *wanted* her—there would be no way she could possibly resist him.

Unfortunately, she also suspected in that moment that willpower was the last thing a man like him engaged in. Especially when it came to things like *wanting.*

"My, you've been patient today," she said as she approached him, telling herself she only imagined the breathlessness she heard lacing her words. Even if she was a little out of breath, it was only because she had been very busy today. Her breathlessness had nothing to do with the fact that Connor looked so...so...so...

Oh, my.

He stood slowly, his entire body seeming to grow and expand with every additional inch of space he claimed, in both height and breadth. At some point during the afternoon, he had discarded his jacket and necktie, and he'd unfastened the top buttons of his shirt to reveal a tantalizing wisp of dark hair beneath. He'd rolled back the cuffs of his white dress shirt, as well, to reveal sun-bronzed, brawny forearms, shadowed with more tantalizing wisps of dark hair, the masculine likes of which Winona had never seen.

Stanley hadn't been an especially virile man. Oh, he'd been masculine enough, and manly about the things most men found interesting. He'd enjoyed sports and had claimed a favorite brand of beer. And although Winona wasn't positive, she was reasonably certain that he had, on occasion, thumbed through her *Victoria's Secret* catalogues with an interest in something other than Christmas shopping for her.

But he hadn't been like Connor. He hadn't exuded a raw masculinity and potent toughness that defied challenge.

For the first time, Winona wondered what, exactly Connor did for a living. All this time she had assumed, thanks to the high-powered business executive suits he wore, that he was, well, a high-powered business executive. Now, however, she began to have her doubts. Wouldn't a high-powered business executive spend much of his day at a desk or computer, or on the telephone or an airplane, or having lunch with other high-powered business executives? And wouldn't such a lifestyle leave a man soft and pale and fleshy?

Yet Connor was hard and dark and lean. He had the appearance and demeanor of a man who spent a good bit of his time doing physical things, especially outdoors. And he didn't seem overly obsessed with the worlds of business and high finance, the way one would assume a high-powered business executive would. On the contrary, he never mentioned business or high finance at all.

Perhaps he thought such conversation would bore her, Winona told herself. Perhaps he was only trying to be polite by always steering the topic of conversation away from himself and what he did for a living. And perhaps he led a health-conscious lifestyle, she thought further. Maybe he spent his weekends outdoors, hiking or rock climbing, or performing some other physical feats of daring-do to negate the sedentary effects of his job. Perhaps that was why he was so physically fit.

Or perhaps he was deliberately misrepresenting himself to her, and pretending to be something he wasn't.

Winona had no idea why such a bizarre thought would leap into her head the way it did just then, and as soon as the peculiar idea materialized, she nudged it aside. It was silly. Connor couldn't possibly be misrepresenting himself or pretending to be something he wasn't, she assured herself. Why would he possibly need or want to? She was being ridiculous.

So, instead, she focused her attention fully on Connor, marveling at the way he seemed to suddenly fill her vision, the way he seemed to suddenly fill her very life. Her heart sped faster and more furiously as she absorbed the sight of him, until she feared it would rattle right up against her ribs and reveal to him just how badly shaken she was by his presence.

And she realized then, too, how very badly she *was* shaken by his presence. More so than she had ever been shaken by anyone else. Including Stanley—the man whom she had intended to marry. The man with whom she had thought she wanted to spend her entire life. The man she had thought she loved. Which could only mean that the feelings she had for Connor were...

Oh, dear.

She stopped herself dead in her tracks, but Connor seemed not to notice her sudden hesitation. Instead he only tossed the last of the Sunday paper onto the table, hooked his hands loosely on his hips and smiled at her. The most dazzling, heart-stopping smile Winona had ever seen.

Oh, yes, she thought as her heart began humming erratically again. She was definitely more firmly under Connor's spell than she had ever been under Stanley's. And something about realizing that made her feel not only panicked, but inexplicably sad.

"You think I've been patient today?" he asked, echoing the comment she could scarcely remember making now, and stirring her from her troubling thoughts. "That's funny, because I don't feel like I'm a particularly patient man." He waiting a telling beat before adding, "Especially not when I'm around you."

Oh, my, Winona thought. Not just because of the sentiment he expressed, but because of the glitter of purpose that ignited in his blue eyes as he said it, giving them the look of a man who fully intended to spend the rest of the day—

Oh, my.

"Right now, for instance," he added, "I'm feeling very impatient. And very..."

He inhaled a deep breath and, for a moment, he only continued to gaze at her in silence. Then, very, very slowly, he released the breath again. He said nothing, however, only kept his attention riveted on her face.

"Very...what?" she finally asked, her voice coming out a bit shallow and hurried.

"Hungry," he finished. "I'm feeling very...hungry."

And why did she suspect that his condition had nothing to do with the need for food?

"There's a, um…a, ah…a, er…" Winona swallowed with some difficulty before she finally managed to get out, "there are a few things left over from lunch that I put in the refrigerator upstairs for my own meals this week. If you're hungry—"

"*Very* hungry," he corrected her.

She nodded nervously. "If you're *very* hungry…" she began again.

"Oh, I'm *starved*," he interrupted her. Once more, though, he somehow made the announcement sound as if it had nothing to do with wanting food.

She nodded again. More nervously. "If you're starved, then…" she said, waiting a moment this time to see if he wanted to add any more clarification. Strangely, she found herself hoping that he would. But he remained silent this time, only continued to gaze at her—hungrily, she couldn't help thinking—and waited to see what she would say. "Then perhaps you'd like something like… Oh, I don't know. I have lovely pasty, for example."

His dark brows shot up in surprise at her announcement, then he rolled his tongue in his cheek. For some reason, Winona received the distinct impression that he was trying very hard not to laugh.

"A, um…a pasty?" he repeated.

She nodded, wondering at the glint of humor that suddenly appeared in his eyes. "Yes. A pasty. Well, actually, I suppose contemporary pronunciation would have the word rhyme with *nasty*. But I prefer the traditional pasty instead."

"Oh, I prefer pasties, too," he told her eagerly. Again, though, Winona felt as if he were laughing at her for some reason. How very odd. "Although there's a lot to be said for nasty, too," he added.

She narrowed her eyes at him suspiciously. What on

earth was he going on about? "All right then," she told him evenly. "Would you like one of my pasties?"

He did, quite literally, bite back a smile at that, and Winona's confusion grew. "Sounds, um...lovely," he told her. "I think I could probably really, you know, wrap my mouth around a pasty right about now. That sounds... really, really good."

And then, suddenly, for some reason, he had to clear his throat. A lot.

How odd, Winona thought again. She hoped he wasn't coming down with a sore throat. It wasn't the cold and flu season yet. Perhaps she should offer him some of the left-over soup, as well.

"There's soup, too," she said helpfully. "My lovely cherry tomato."

"Your...cherry...tomato?"

Goodness, his hearing must be clouded, too, she thought. He had to repeat everything she said, as if he were having trouble. And what a strange voice he was repeating it in, too.

A bit louder this time, she repeated, "Yes. Cherry. Tomato. Are you interested?"

He held up a hand, palm out, in a silent bid for her to stop, and now she could very easily see that he was indeed trying not to laugh. "No, thank you," he told her. "I'm just really looking forward to the getting that, uh, that pasty in my mouth."

Winona narrowed her eyes at him once more. He was doing it again, she thought. Making suggestive remarks that she didn't understand. She didn't know *why* they were suggestive, only that they *were*. She could tell by the way he was voicing them that he was thinking about something completely different from what she was thinking herself.

And, somehow she knew whatever was going through his mind was sexual in nature. She could tell *that* by the way her own body caught fire at hearing his roughly uttered words and seeing the spark of fire in his eyes. For all Winona's expounding on the importance of virtue and chastity and decency, sometimes, she thought, it simply did not pay to be sexually inexperienced.

"Fine," she said evenly. She turned her back on Connor then, and began to walk forward. Over her shoulder, she told him, "If you'll just follow me upstairs to my private quarters, then I'll ply you with the plumpest, hottest pasty I have at my disposal."

She heard him utter a strangled little sound at her announcement, but all he said in reply was, "Oh, Winona, my...mouth...is watering already."

Connor couldn't remember the last time he had enjoyed a meal as much as he enjoyed his Sunday dinner sitting in Winona Thornbury's abundantly decorated, outrageously feminine—and very private—quarters. Of course, it wasn't often that a woman like her offered a man like him one of her hot, plump pasties, or carried on about her cherry tomatoes, but that was beside the point.

The point was that she had been so innocent while voicing the offer of her hot, plump pasty and her cherry tomatoes. She really had been. Nobody could fake that kind of naïveté. And Connor just loved that. He loved her innocence, her ingenuousness. He loved that she'd been completely unconscious of the fact that she had been tossing double entendres his way by the handful. He loved it that she was obviously so inexperienced when it came to matters of a sexual nature.

And he loved her hot, plump pasties, too.

Okay, enough of the pasty jokes, he told himself as he sat back in his chair to watch Winona daintily pour tea from a dainty china teapot into his dainty china cup. His feelings for her, he knew, were anything but a joke, even if they were completely bewildering.

Normally Connor didn't go for innocent and ingenuous

and inexperienced. Normally, he liked his women to be as sexually sophisticated as he was himself. He had a strong sex drive. And he liked for that sex drive to be satisfied quickly and intensely and repeatedly. He didn't have the time or inclination—or the patience, for that matter—to teach someone about what pleased him. He wanted women who already knew how to do that—in spades.

But with Winona... For some reason he felt just the opposite. He liked it that she seemed to have very little knowledge of what went on between a man and a woman. He liked it that she didn't appear to have an extensive collection of lovers in her past. And he liked it that, in spite of all her innocence, ingenuousness and inexperience, she still seemed to catch fire whenever he came within a hundred feet of her.

Hell, he just liked Winona, period. He liked her a lot. And he was decent enough to admit, now, that he had been completely wrong about her from the beginning. Clearly, she had no knowledge of the fact that an illegal operation was running like clockwork right under her nose, in the very business whose reputation she strove to keep stellar. And she certainly wasn't the ruthless madam of a high-class prostitution ring.

What she was, Connor now realized, was a nice, old-fashioned girl. One who couldn't possibly see the illicit goings-on in her restaurant, because she was totally ignorant of the dark side of life. One who lived hopelessly in a world of manners and courtesy that was as old-fashioned as she was herself. One who celebrated a time when femininity and virtue were both highly prized attributes in a woman. One who honored her own femininity and virtue by being absolutely comfortable with both.

One who was being grossly taken advantage of by a man who was being anything but honest with her.

The moment the thought materialized, Connor pushed it brusquely away. He'd take care of that soon, he promised himself. He would. As soon as it was within his power to do so, he would tell Winona the truth, and explain why he had been forced to deceive her the way he had been deceiving her. The minute they wrapped up this investigation, he would spill all. Somehow he would make her understand that he'd had no choice but to mislead her. Somehow she would see his side of things, and she wouldn't be mad. Somehow everything would work out.

Because there was something else Connor had become aware of recently. He'd become aware of the fact that he didn't want his time with Winona to end. Not yet, anyway. He liked being a part of her life, enjoyed her company, wanted to get to know her better. Lots better. He'd never met a woman like her before, and he had a strange, inexplicable desire to learn more about her. Her. A nice, old-fashioned girl. An innocent, ingenuous, inexperienced—

The thought got stuck in his brain this time, because he finally realized what he was saying about Winona. Innocent. Ingenuous. Inexperienced.

Completely innocent? he wondered suddenly. Utterly ingenuous? *Totally* inexperienced?

As in…*virginal?*

Was that possible? Was it possible that Winona Thornbury had never been with a man? She was a thirty-eight-year-old woman, he immediately reminded himself. Of course it wasn't possible. What woman could arrive at the age of thirty-eight, in this day and age, and not have experienced that? Even a nice, old-fashioned girl had natural urges and desires. Hell, Connor could tell by the way she looked at him that she had needs. Profound needs, at that. Even all buttoned up and battened down, Winona was obviously a passionate woman. There was no way she would have let those passions go unsatisfied all these years, would she?

Would she?

Then again, there was no denying that she acted so…

And she seemed so… And she gave the impression of being so…

"So, Winona," he said suddenly, startling her enough that a bit of tea sloshed over the side of the cup as she poured some for herself, "tell me more about yourself."

She finished filling her cup, then sat down and reached for her linen napkin, using it to dab at the small brown stain that had appeared on the linen tablecloth during the accident. For a long time she focused intently on removing the immovable stain, and Connor wondered if she was going to pretend she hadn't heard him. He was about to ask the question again—because, dammit, he intended to satisfy himself one way or another tonight—when she finally surrendered to the stain and refolded her napkin, placing it carefully beside her plate.

Then, as she reached for the sugar bowl and took the lid off, she asked, "Tell you what about myself? I told you all about myself Monday."

Well, not *quite* everything, Connor thought. She'd totally bypassed her sexual history, for instance. Of course, it had just been their first date. Then again, lots of first dates covered past sexual history these days, due to the fact that sex was a lot more dangerous now than it used to be.

He shrugged, feigning nonchalance. He couldn't very well ask her point-blank how many lovers she'd had, could he? Nor could he conceive of a polite way to phrase the question, *So…anybody popped your cherry yet or what?*

So instead, he only hedged, "How is it that a beautiful, vivacious, intelligent, virtuous—" okay, so he couldn't quite leave the innocent thing alone "—woman like you hasn't been snatched up by some guy a long time ago?"

Instead of being flattered by the question and responding with a knowing little smile, Winona flinched so violently that she shot a spoonful of sugar halfway across the dining room table. And it was big table, too, Connor couldn't help noting. Which meant she'd put some real effort into that flinch.

"I...I...I...I don't know what you...what you mean," she stammered. And she blushed furiously as she stammered, obviously *very* uncomfortable with the subject matter. The impression was only magnified when she hastily began trying to sweep up the sugar with one hand and succeeded only in scattering it about the table even worse than it was already scattered.

In spite of her obvious discomfort, though, Connor persisted. "I mean how come you've never been married?" he asked again, more specifically this time.

She glanced up at him quickly, then just as hastily dropped her gaze back down to the sugar she was so ineffectually trying to gather. "Who, um, who says I've never been married?"

Whoa, Connor thought. This was news. How had they missed a husband during their investigation of Winona Thornbury? And why did the realization that there was one—or, at the very least, had been one—bother him so damned much?

"You're married?" he asked, his voice sounding flat and empty, even to his own ears.

She threw him another one of those hasty glances, then went back to work on the sugar. This time, she actually managed to collect a few granules, which she flicked impolitely into her coffee, clearly so annoyed now by the conversation that she had completely forgotten her manners.

"No, I'm not married," she told him.

And just like that, the Earth began to rotate normally on its axis again, and Connor remembered to breathe.

She continued to focus on the sugar as she added, "Do you honestly think I would have been...kissing you...this week if I were a married woman? You did, after all, just say that I was virtuous."

Yeah, but are you a virgin? he wanted to demand. Instead he told her, "No, I don't think you would have been kissing me if you were married. You just threw me for a loop there for a minute, that's all."

"I do sincerely apologize for the loop throwing," she said, obviously trying to evade the subject. And she still wasn't looking him in the eye.

"Are you divorced?" Connor asked.

She didn't even look up at him this time. "No. I don't believe in divorce. I only believe in marrying out of love. Real love. True love. Love that never dies. Marrying for that kind of love makes divorce unnecessary."

Oh, man, he thought. That must mean... Very softly he asked, "You're widowed?"

She shook her head and sighed heavily. "No. I'm sorry. I didn't mean to mislead you. I've never been married, Connor."

He hesitated only a moment before asking, "Because you've never been in love? Real love? True love?"

Very, very softly now, she said, "I didn't say that." After a moment—and another one of those hasty glances in his general direction—she added, with a bit more fortitude, "I've been in love. I've just never been married."

"Then why...?"

"The not-being-married part wasn't through any choice of my own," she told him. "Had things worked out the way I'd planned for them to work out years ago, I would indeed be a married woman right now."

And why did she actually sound sad about such a prospect, instead of wistful? Connor wondered. She'd just said she'd been in love. Didn't that mean she wished she'd married the guy? Who else would she have been in love with? And why would it make her sad to be married to him now?

"I don't understand," he told her.

"I was engaged to be married once," she replied simply. At her frankly offered announcement, the Earth seemed to tip again beneath Connor. It was the strangest sensation. Although nothing in his immediate reality had shifted, at the realization that Winona had once loved another man and had intended to tie her life to his forever, everything seemed to change.

And then Connor's phrasing struck him. Winona had loved *another* man, he repeated to himself. That made it sound as if he considered her fiancé to be a rival of sorts. And that made no sense. Not only was the other guy obviously no longer a part of her life, but why should Connor consider him a rival? A rival for what? Her affections? He still wasn't sure he wanted her affections. Certainly not the way that other guy had had them. Yeah, Connor wanted Winona. But there was no way he wanted to *marry* her.

He shook the dilemma off quite literally and turned his attention back to her. "You were going to get married to someone?" he asked.

She nodded and gazed blindly down into her coffee. "That was my plan, yes."

"So what happened?"

She finally did meet Connor's gaze then, dead-on. But her expression offered nothing as to what she might be thinking or feeling, and all he could do was gaze back in silence.

"I believe," she said quietly, "that the colloquial phrase for what happened would be, 'He dumped me.'"

Connor's mouth dropped open in astonishment at that. *He* had dumped *her?* he thought. How was that possible? What the hell kind of idiot man dumped a woman like Winona? That was nuts. "He what?" he asked.

"Stanley left me for another woman."

The information still wouldn't quite gel in Connor's brain. What other woman? How could there even *be* another woman when a man had Winona Thornbury warming his bed? Then again, she still hadn't said anything to suggest she wasn't a virgin, so maybe she *hadn't* warmed ol'

Stanley's bed. Maybe that had been ol' Stanley's problem with the relationship in the first place. Still, even at that, a man would have to be crazy to let a woman like Winona get away. Hey, there was a lot more to a relationship than hot sex, after all.

And Connor could not *believe* he had just thought such a thing.

Even more amazing, he couldn't believe he believed it. But he suddenly realized that he did. He believed it most sincerely. For the first time in his life, Connor could honestly see how there might be more to a relationship than hot sex. Because here he was, having a nice time with Winona—having had a nice time with Winona on more than one occasion now—and they hadn't even come close to having sex, hot or otherwise.

Wow. What a concept. Who knew?

As he basked in this newly discovered knowledge, and before he could say anything else and without even having to ask for details, Winona suddenly started talking again, about the very thing Connor found most interesting—her relationship with the jerk who had dumped her. He settled back in his chair to listen. 'Cause this, he had to hear.

Eight

"I met Stanley when I was twenty-six," she said, turning her attention now back to her teacup. "We dated for three years before becoming engaged. Then, one week before the wedding, he left me."

Okay, so that answered one question, Connor thought. Probably. Because he couldn't imagine anyone dating for three years and not becoming physically intimate. Certainly they would have made love once they were engaged, wouldn't they? Even a nice, old-fashioned girl wouldn't have held out once she had a ring, albeit engagement only, on her finger, right? Winona must not be totally inexperienced, if she'd been engaged to the guy.

Still, this was Winona they were talking about, he reminded himself. So until she spelled it out for him, Connor couldn't be certain about anything.

He wanted to say something, at least offer some vague platitude in response, because he honestly wasn't sure what else to say. But Winona began speaking again, offering more details, so he only remained silent and listened.

"Stanley was very special to me," she said.

Okay, so maybe that was one detail he could have lived without.

"He was my...my first. Lover, I mean."

And maybe that detail wasn't as important as Connor had originally thought it, either, even if she had just spelled out exactly what he'd wanted to know. Because the thread of jealousy that wound through him at hearing it was a totally unfamiliar, totally unpleasant thing for him to feel. He'd never been jealous of any woman's previous sexual encounters. Not until now. But the thought of Winona with another man—yes, *another* man, dammit—even if she had met him years before Connor had even entered the picture... Well, it just felt lousy, that was all.

"I'd never...with anyone before him," she continued. "And I haven't...with anyone since, either. Even with Stanley, I didn't... I couldn't... Until we were practically married. It was three weeks before the wedding when I finally... When we finally..."

"I understand, Winona," Connor said. "If you're uncomfortable talking about it..."

"No, it isn't that," she said quickly, glancing up to look at Connor for the first time since she began talking about her broken engagement. And she seemed to be as surprised by her comment as Connor was. "In fact, I want to tell you about it," she told him. "I think I need to tell you about it. I think it's important that you understand."

"Understand what?" he asked.

She eyed him levelly. "How important that kind of relationship is to me. I can't be casual about...you know."

"Sex?" he asked frankly.

She squeezed her eyes shut tight, and two bright spots of color darkened her cheeks. "Yes," she said softly. "That. It isn't in my nature to be casual about it."

"I didn't think you were casual about it," he told her.

"I know. But you and I are of entirely different generations, Connor, and I know you feel differently about this than I do. Stanley and I were practically... We'd made a commitment to each other. What I, at least, considered to be a life-long commitment. I thought he and I were going to be together forever. Otherwise, I never would have..."

"So what happened?" Connor asked. He realized now that he very much wanted to hear the end of the story, even with the presence of that idiot Stanley in it.

"Stanley bought a computer," she said.

Connor waited for her to continue, to offer some kind of clarification for her comment, because he sure as hell couldn't see any connection. When she offered nothing more, though, he spurred gently, "And that would be significant because..."

Winona sighed heavily and turned her attention back to the spilled sugar. Instead of trying to clean it up, however, she only began to drag her index finger through it, making an idle design on the tablecloth. She watched the movement of her own hand blindly as she said, "He went online and found an entire world on the Internet that didn't exist in Bloomington."

"What kind of world?" Connor asked. Hell, what could ol' Stanley have found online that he didn't already have right here?

"He met a woman in a chat room," Winona said.

Oh, *that* kind of world, Connor thought. Yeah, a guy would be hard-pressed to find that world here in Bloomington. Unless he went to Winona's restaurant, of course, and picked up one of the phones. But that was neither here nor there.

"What I didn't realize when Stanley and I finally became intimate," she continued, "was that he had met this woman online, and was having... I guess you'd call it a cyber affair with her. I think it was what made him press for a more..."

She cleared her throat delicately. "A more…physical relationship with me. She brought out feelings in him…needs in him…that he wasn't able to satisfy with her, because she was in another state. So he turned to me for that, even though he knew I wanted to wait until we were married."

Something chilly crept up Connor's spine. "He didn't force you to…?"

"No," she said hastily. "It wasn't like that at all. I did want for Stanley and me to get more…to have…that. I was looking forward to it. I'd just really wanted to wait until our wedding night. But one evening he came to my apartment, and he brought me flowers, and he cooked me dinner, and he played soft music, and we danced, and…" She sighed almost wistfully. "He seduced me. It was actually very romantic. And quite pleasant."

That was another detail Connor could have lived without. But he said nothing that might have halted her story. Instead, he only waited to hear the rest.

"Oh, yes," she continued quietly. "It was very pleasant indeed."

Yeah, yeah, yeah, Connor thought. Just get on with it.

"In fact, it was *so* pleasant," Winona said, "that it happened several times after that, and really, I discovered so many things about myself during those two weeks. If nothing else, Stanley taught me—"

"So what went wrong?" Connor interrupted. There were just some details best left out, he thought.

Winona looked at him with some confusion for a moment, then, "Oh," she said. "Oh, yes. I'm sorry. As I said, by then he'd met a woman online and was carrying on with her. I suppose he'd hoped that when the two of us became physically intimate, it might satisfy the…urges…she had aroused in him. Evidently, though, he needed something more."

Idiot, Connor thought.

"He needed something I couldn't give him. I wasn't enough for him."

Idiot, idiot, Connor thought.

"Because one morning a week before the wedding, I woke up to find a note tucked into my mailbox. It was from Stanley. At first, I thought it was going to be some little love note from him, telling me how much he adored me, and how complete I'd made him feel. Instead, he told me that what he and I shared wasn't at all... Well, let's just say I didn't live up to his expectations."

Idiot, idiot, idiot, Connor thought.

"And he said he was sorry," she went on, "but he was moving to Racine, Wisconsin, to pursue a new life with his cyber love. I never heard from him again. I assume they lived happily—or something—ever after. As for me, I had to call nearly a hundred wedding guests and explain what had happened, then return sixty-five gifts that had already arrived."

"Oh, Winona..."

She closed her eyes for a moment, then opened them. "It wasn't a completely horrible experience. I learned some very important things from Stanley."

"Yeah, number one being that he was a complete jerk," Connor offered.

She smiled a bit sadly. "Yes, that was indeed the first lesson. The second was that what could...could...*ignite* between a man and a woman completely surpassed anything I could have ever imagined. And the third, most important, lesson was that one about the cow."

Okay, now Connor was hopelessly lost. "The, um, the cow?" he asked.

She nodded. "About how men don't buy it when they can get the milk for free."

"Oh, *that* cow," Connor said. "Actually, that's a misconception. Men will buy just about anything if you get them in the right frame of mind."

She said nothing in response to that, only gazed at the spilled sugar and her quickly cooling tea for several long, silent moments. Then suddenly, as if she were snapping out of a dream, she sat up straight and looked Connor right in the eye.

"Goodness," she said. "I don't know what's come over me tonight, to be discussing my relationship with Stanley. It's not exactly a polite topic of conversation, is it?"

Maybe not, Connor thought. But it was definitely an interesting one.

"I apologize for being so rude," she told him.

"You weren't being rude, Winona," he said, smiling. "You just needed someone to talk to."

She smiled back. "Thank you."

"For what?"

"For understanding."

Connor shook his head. "Hey, I don't understand anything about this. The fact that Stanley preferred some cyber babe over you, Winona... The fact that he preferred *any* woman over you..." He paid her the great honor of being completely baffled by Stanley's choice. "It makes no sense to me, that's all. And if Stanley felt that way," he continued, "then there was no way he was the right man for you. Hell, he wasn't a man at all."

She blushed becomingly, and her smiled brightened. "Well, I do agree that he wasn't the man for me. In hindsight, I'm glad I didn't marry him. He obviously didn't love me the way he should have. And it's not as though I'm pining away for him, is it? I've moved on."

But did she still love him? Connor wondered. She had, after all, said she would only marry out of real, true love. Love that lasted forever. Was that what she had felt for the dishonorable Stanley? It must have been, if she'd agreed to marry him. And if that was the case, was she lost for good?

But lost to whom? Connor asked himself. Once again, he'd chosen a strange way to collect his thoughts.

"Would you like to take our tea out onto the balcony?" she asked suddenly.

Her question dispelled the tumult of confusion that was wheeling through his head, something for which Connor was grateful, quite frankly. "I didn't know you had a balcony," he said. He had, after all, surveyed the exterior of her home quite extensively, and he couldn't recall a balcony anywhere.

"Well, I suppose 'balcony' is being generous," she said with a smile. "But I do have a little sitting area off my room that's nice for enjoying afters."

The word *afters* probably would have registered on Connor in a salacious way if it weren't for the fact that he never really heard anything after the words *my room*. As far as he was concerned, any chance to get a glimpse of Winona's more personal side was way welcome. And he did recall now a little decklike structure, barely big enough for two, extending from the back corner of the building. That must have been what she was talking about.

"Sure," he said agreeably. "That sounds great. There's supposed to be a full moon tonight, isn't there?"

She nodded. "It should be lovely."

It certainly should, he thought.

He followed her from the dining room through the rest of her home, glimpsing parts of it for the very first time. There was a generously sized living room—furnished in more of that Victorian excess style that she seemed to favor—a small office, only marginally cluttered, what appeared to be a sitting room of sorts, a spare room and, finally, Winona's bedroom.

Like the rest of the house, it was abundantly furnished with floral fabrics and hooked rugs with flower designs spanning the hardwood flooring, and lace curtains fluttering over the windows. The walls were covered with dried flower wreaths, and oil-on-canvas paintings of fair maidens gazing pensively out over grassy meadows. A small writing desk and stool were tucked into one corner, an ornate rocking chair sat in another. Two French doors on the opposite side of the room were closed and covered with more lace, but Winona promptly crossed to them and pulled them open, revealing what was indeed a small, covered sitting area beyond, just large enough for an economy-size wicker chair and settee, both covered with, inescapably, flowered cushions.

But that wasn't what caught most of Connor's attention just then. No, what caught most of his attention just then was the antique sleigh bed of indeterminate size that was, without question, the focal point of the room. At least it was Connor's focal point. Because for some reason, he couldn't quite bring himself to look away from it. Not quite double, not quite single, it would, nonetheless, accommodate two people, provided they slept closely together. Really closely together. Really, *really* closely together.

Gee, funny how the room had grown so much warmer after Winona had opened the doors onto a cool evening. Even though he could feel the kiss of an early autumn breeze on his face, Connor suddenly felt as if he'd walked right into an oven. How odd.

He realized then that Winona had already stepped outside and had placed her cup on the wide railing near the settee. She still stood, though, obviously reluctant to sit on either piece of furniture. Connor sensed her dilemma. If she sat on the settee, she might give him the impression that she wanted to be close to him, which he would naturally take as a romantic overture, and, it went without saying, he would take advantage of it. And if she sat on the chair, she might give him the impression that she feared being close to him, something he would naturally interpret as her desire to be close to him, which he would naturally take as a romantic overture, and, it went without saying, he would take advantage of it.

He smiled. Gee. The night was looking up. Big time.

As he silently crossed the bedroom toward the French doors, Connor couldn't help wondering if Winona were regretting her invitation to have him join her on her balcony. Gosh, he hoped not. Because he was really looking forward to seeing how things were going to turn out.

"It's nice out here," he said as he joined her outside. He couldn't help noticing that she jumped a little bit when he said it. Oh, he did so love having this effect on her.

"Yes," she said shortly. "It is. Nice. Out here, I mean."

Hmm, he thought. He'd reduced her to single syllables. This was getting interesting. Then again, he wasn't exactly being polysyllabic himself now, was he? He smiled. This was definitely getting interesting.

He set his own cup down next to hers, then turned his body to face her, leaning his hip on the railing. A good foot of space separated them, but he could still inhale the sweet lilac scent of her. And in the pale-yellow light that spilled out onto the deck from her bedroom, he could see the way the breeze plucked strands of gold from the tightly wound bun at the back of her head and danced them around her face. He could see the elegant line of her jaw, the blush of pink on her cheek, the berry sheen of her plump mouth.

She was exquisitely beautiful, he couldn't help thinking. Smart, funny, womanly and genuinely sweet. She was everything he should be running away from. Instead, he only wanted to pull her close.

Winona knew immediately after Connor joined her outside that it had been a very bad idea to invite him out here. Honestly, she had no idea what had possessed her to extend such an offer in the first place. This balcony was her private abode, the one place in her house where she could come and feel truly alone and at peace. But now Connor had invaded this place, at her invitation, and she didn't know what to do.

How could she have told him all those things about her relationship with Stanley? How could she have revealed such intimate details of her life to him? She'd never told anyone about her experiences with her ex-fiancé, had never even *wanted* to tell anyone about them. Yet she had spilled it all to Connor without the least provocation. And she simply did not know why.

She'd only known that she did need to tell him, that it was important for some reason that he know how seriously she took such a relationship. Perhaps, deep down, she knew where she and Connor were headed, knew the two of them were destined to end up in the same way she and Stanley had. She knew that, because the feelings she had for Connor made those she'd had for Stanley seem tepid and unreal. She had thought that she loved Stanley. She knew now that she had not. Because now…

Now she knew what it meant to love someone. As crazy as it seemed, at some point over the last few weeks, perhaps before she'd even spoken to him, Winona had fallen in love with Connor Montgomery.

There. She had admitted it. She knew it made no sense. She knew it was foolish. She knew it was unfounded. She knew it was mad. But she also knew it was real. And she knew it would last forever. And that was why she had needed to let him know what kind of woman she was. That was why it had been so important for her to make Connor understand what it meant for her to become as deeply involved with a man as she had with Stanley.

And now Connor did understand. She hoped. Surely he realized now that she would only make love with a man who was committed to her forever. And he knew she would only make that commitment to someone she truly loved. Therefore, if the two of them did follow what was happening between them to its natural conclusion, Connor would know that she loved him. Deeply. Truly. Irrevocably. And she knew—somehow, she *knew*—that he would be honorable enough to respect that.

He would be honorable enough to only make love to her

if he truly loved her, too. If she offered herself to Connor now, after all she had revealed to him, she would be telling him, without words, that she loved him and would remain committed to him forever. And because he understood that now, after all she had revealed to him, he would only accept her offer—would only make love to her—if he could make the same commitment to her in return. Surely he understood that now, she told herself. Surely, she had made that clear. Surely he didn't need for her to spell it out.

Surely, if he made love to her tonight, it would be because he felt the same way for her that she did for him. It would be because he loved her, too. Deeply. Truly. Irrevocably. Otherwise, he wouldn't accept her offer, and he would walk away.

She was still telling herself that when she suddenly felt a soft touch on her face, the merest brush of Connor's fingertips over her cheek. Startled, she turned to face him, and found him gazing at her intently, his blue eyes filled with something she was almost afraid to consider. He understood, she thought as she looked into his eyes. He really did understand everything she had told him, without telling him in so many words. He knew that she loved him. She could see it in his eyes. And she saw something else there, too, something that told her he—

"You are so beautiful," he said softly, almost reverently. "So..." But his voice trailed off before he completed the thought.

As Winona stood there gazing at him in silence, he lifted his other hand now, turning it to brush his bent knuckles along the line of her jaw. Involuntarily she let her eyes flutter closed, so that she might enjoy the sweetness of the gesture more keenly. And when she did, something inside her that she hadn't even realized she was restraining broke free.

A swirl of something wild and wonderful seemed to hum through her entire body as he touched her, coiling tight in some dark place deep inside. Her lips parted to enable her to better breathe, but instead of aiding herself, she somehow only felt more breathless. Again and again, Connor dragged his knuckles tenderly over her cheekbone, along her jaw, down along the column of her throat, until Winona didn't think she could tolerate the sensation any longer. When she finally opened her eyes, it was to find him gazing at her now as if she were the strangest puzzle he'd ever seen. A puzzle he couldn't wait to unlock.

Then he was bending toward her, dipping his head to hers. She knew he was going to kiss her, and she told herself to make him stop, because everything was happening much too quickly. Instead, she tipped her head back a bit and reached a hand toward him, meeting him a little better than halfway.

She knew immediately as she curled her fingers into the soft fabric of his shirt that this kiss wasn't going to be like the others they had shared. And the moment his mouth covered hers, she saw that she was right.

Where before he had only grazed her lips briefly once, twice, thrice, with his own, now he covered her mouth wholly with his in a kiss that was at once generous and possessive. Brazenly he pressed his entire body to hers, looping one arm around her waist to bend her backward as he deepened the kiss. The hand that had so gently grazed her face cupped her jaw firmly now, his thumb cradling her chin as he tipped her head back further still.

Winona gasped at the intensity of his embrace, but instead of retreating from him, she only tightened her hold on his shirt with one hand and pressed her other palm to his shoulder, grasping firmly the hard, heated musculature she encountered there. He was so large, so solid, so... so...so *much,* she thought. She told herself she should be intimidated by him, frightened of him, even. But she was neither of those things. In spite of the tumultuousness of the moment, a strange sort of calm washed over her, as if she were in exactly the place she was meant to be, at exactly the right time. In spite of her apprehensions, right here, right now, with Connor, felt like the most natural place in the world for her.

Unable to tolerate not touching him, Winona curved one hand around the warm skin of his nape, and threaded the fingers of the other up into his straight, silky hair. He seemed to like the sensation, because he accelerated the kiss even more, sinking his tongue into her mouth to taste her more deeply. Winona uttered a wild little sound at the invasion, curling her fingers more tightly over him in response. Connor responded by pulling her body hard against his own, then tilted his head to one side to facilitate his penetration even more.

He seemed to get lost in the kiss after that. Or maybe Winona was the one who got lost. She never was quite sure. Gradually, though, everything around her—everything inside her—seemed to shift and change and meld with Connor. There was only him. Only her. Only the two of them. She wasn't sure how long they stood so entwined, kissing, caressing, exploring each other more completely. But during that time, Winona felt as if she joined with Connor in ways she had never joined with another human being. He seemed to become a part of her, and she of him. And indeed there were times when she wasn't sure which of them was touching her, or him, or them, or…

And then she ceased to think at all, responded only to the myriad sensations unfolding in her mind and body. She dropped a hand to his chest, splaying her fingers open wide over his heart, and was comforted by the ragged, erratic pulse that hammered hard against her fingertips. He was every bit as shaken and tautly strung as she was herself, she thought. And somehow, that made everything all right.

She reacted instinctively after that, moving her hand lower, inverting it so that her fingers tipped downward, pressing the heel of her palm against his rock solid abdomen. She liked the way he felt, the way his body was so much different from her own. He was hard where she was soft, his body solid where hers was giving. They complemented each other so nicely, so naturally, so perfectly.

When she curled her fingers more insistently into his lean torso, he dropped one hand to her waist. He rested the side of his palm on her hip, hooking his thumb around front, settling it at the base of her rib cage. And all the while he kept kissing her, tasting her, consuming her. Winona told herself she should retreat, should pull away, should put a stop to things before they went too far.

But the way he was touching her and kissing her felt so good, she thought. Having him close this way generated things inside her she'd never felt before. She didn't want to retreat or pull away or a put a stop to things. Not yet. There would be time for that soon, she told herself. She would halt him—and herself—before things got out of hand. But right now she only wanted to know more.

His hand at her waist crept higher then, skimming lightly over her rib cage, until he settled his hand just beneath her breast, framing its plump fullness in the el-shape created by the position of his thumb and forefinger. Winona's heart raced at the intimacy of the touch, but instead of shrinking away from him, she automatically arched her body forward. Connor responded by growling something low and incoherent, then covering her breast completely with his hand, closing his fingers possessively over her.

Winona jerked her mouth from his at the contact, gasping her surprise. When she looked up at him, she saw him panting for breath, his cheeks ruddy from his passion, his pupils dilated in need. He met her gaze unflinchingly, but he didn't remove his hand. Instead he only closed his fingers even more possessively over her, pressed his palm more intimately against her. Winona's breathing, too, was rapid and irregular, and she imagined her face reflected her emotions as his did. For a long moment neither of them moved. Connor kept his hand right where he had placed it, and Winona did nothing to remove it.

Then, in one deft, smooth move, he opened his fingers and closed them again, more tightly this time, grasping her breast even more firmly. Winona's eyes fluttered closed, and she twisted the fabric of his shirt in her hands. Somehow she pulled him closer to her, when she'd thought he was as close as he could be. She sensed, more than saw, Connor dip his head toward her again, only this time he buried his face in the tender, fragrant skin of her neck.

As he palmed and petted her breast, he dragged his open mouth along the column of her throat, and Winona threw her head backward to facilitate his actions. The next thing she knew, he had his hand tangled in her hair, freeing the chignon she had taken such pains to arrange that morning. As her unbound tresses cascaded down toward her waist, she heard him murmur something low and lusty, words she couldn't quite make out, even if she understood their meaning instinctively.

The hand at her breast moved in a different way then, and through the haze of desire that had enveloped her, Winona gradually became aware of the fact that Connor was unbuttoning her dress. Without questioning her actions, she reached for the cameo at her throat and unpinned it, tucking the brooch blindly into her pocket before curving her hands over his shoulders once again. When he'd freed the buttons past her waist, he shoved the garment from her shoulders, skimming it down over her body until it pooled at her feet.

She should have felt shocked and embarrassed, Winona told herself. But the white cotton slip she wore beneath the dress covered nearly as much of her as the dress itself had. Nevertheless, it was one less barrier between them, and she felt the heat of his hand more keenly as he placed it over her breast again, grazing his thumb over the ripe peak in a slow, methodical, maddening, circle.

''Winona,'' he whispered as he pressed his forehead to

hers, "is what I think is going to happen really going to happen?" His voice was coarse and indelicate and needful and, oh, so very seductive.

She hesitated before answering, not sure what she should say. She wondered again if he truly understood what it would mean for her to let happen what he was suggesting. She wondered if he was willing to make the commitment to her that she had already made to him, however nebulously.

"I...I don't know," she told him honestly.

He pulled back a bit, gazing down at her face, his expression telling her nothing of what he might be feeling. There was something in his eyes, though, that made her feel hopeful. She wasn't sure why.

"Do you want it to happen?" he asked her.

Unable to lie to him, she slowly nodded. "Yes. I do."

"I do, too."

She swallowed hard. "You know what it means to me, Connor," she said. "You know what kind of woman I am."

His eyes never left hers as he replied immediately, and very resolutely, "Yes. I do."

"And you still want to..."

"Yes," he said. "I want to make love to you, Winona. Very much. More than anything I've ever wanted in my life. Do you want to make love to me?"

Her heart hammered hard in her chest, and the breath left her lungs in one long, low whoosh of air. He hadn't said it, she thought. He hadn't told her he loved her. He hadn't made any commitment to her. But he understood, right? she thought. He must understand. He must know that she demanded a life-long commitment before she would agree to—

"Yes," she said without thinking any further. One could only do so much thinking, she thought. Eventually one must act. And one must grab for one's happiness wherever it might lie.

So she lifted a hand to cup it over his rough jaw, and fastened her gaze to his. "Yes," she told him. "I want to make love with you."

Nine

For one long moment Connor only continued to gaze down at her in silence. Then, very slowly, he bent his body to the side, and reached his hand down toward the hem of her slip. Winona watched with a detached sort of fascination as he bunched the edge of the white garment in his bronzed fingers, wrapping the supple cotton resolutely around his hand again and again, until the garment was pulled taut against her skin. Then slowly, leisurely, oh...so erotically, he began to tug the fabric upward, until Winona could feel the caress of sweet September air on her naked calves.

Then yet higher, over her heated, sensitive flesh, until her knees and thighs felt the cool nuzzle of autumn, as well. When the fabric rose higher still, toward her hips, she turned her face to his, telling herself that this was insane, that they shouldn't do it, and that she must order him to stop. But he dipped his head to hers and kissed her, fiercely, possessively, druggingly, until Winona forgot entirely whatever she had intended to say.

In fact, as he deepened the kiss even more, invading her mouth with his tongue again to taste her as completely as before, she scarcely remembered who or what she was. She scarcely felt mortal at all. No, she was someone else, some-*thing* else, some sentient, fantastical being whose reason for existence was simply to feel the pleasure that Connor Montgomery wrought.

And what pleasure he wrought as he pulled her closer, drawing her slip higher now, up over her thighs and hips, until he had bundled it at her waist. With one arm roped resolutely about her middle, he hauled her close, until her body was completely flush against his. Winona gasped at the utter ownership in the gesture, but inside she thrilled at how desperately he wanted her.

She curled her fingers over his shoulders as he held her, then gasped once more when he dropped his free hand to splay it open over the soft cotton panties hugging her bottom. Then he began drawing rapid circles with eager fingertips over the thin fabric and her delicate flesh. The friction of the sensation sent something inside Winona churning uncontrollably. And when he curved his palm comfortably, confidently, over the lower curve of one buttock, she nearly lost her breath completely. *He shouldn't,* she thought, *he couldn't…he wouldn't…*

He did.

In that next moment, as he bent his body forward over hers, taking even greater possession of the kiss, of Winona, Connor tucked his fingers under the lacy waistband of her panties, spreading his fingers open wide over the bare flesh beneath.

The sensation that shot through her then was filled with fire, with need, with hunger. Never in her life had she experienced such an intense rapacity, such an acute urgency, such a profound desire. Never had she wanted anything—anyone—the way she wanted Connor in that moment.

The fingers cupping over her fanny clutched tighter then,

kneading her sensitive flesh intimately, emphatically, parting and exploring the sensitive cleft between before scooting lower still. Winona's knees buckled beneath her, and it was only with great effort—and the arm still roped around her waist—that she was able to remain standing. And all the while, his fingers crept lower, parting, pushing, invading, until they pulled down the chaste cotton panties to bare her bottom completely.

He dragged the scant garment down over her legs, and Winona obediently stepped out of it. Then he straightened, moving his hand this time between their bodies, skimming it up under her slip, over and between her legs, toward the very heart of her femininity. Before she could utter a word to object—not that she wanted to object, necessarily, but she thought that she probably should—Connor moved his fingers over her, into her, zealously fingering the damp folds of flesh he encountered there. Winona cried out at the contact, clutching him more fiercely, her entire body quaking as he creased her, stroked her, caressed her…and then penetrated her.

And when he did that, Winona knew it was over for her. Because the moment Connor possessed her in such a way, she knew it would never be enough. Not for him, and certainly not for her. With that skilled invasion, he unleashed in her something that had, until now, remained imprisoned, and there would be no way to corral the creature until she had received satisfaction. And satisfaction, Winona knew, would only come in the form of Connor. She would not be satisfied until the two of them finished what they had, perhaps foolishly, begun.

She parted her lips to say something, though truly, she knew not what, but Connor covered her mouth again with his and tasted her deeply, thoroughly, until she went limp in his arms. The twin penetrations of tongue and finger made her entire body shudder in response, and she could only cling to him, her fists curled in the fabric of his shirt, as he continued with his onslaught.

Again and again he kissed her, again and again he moved his fingers over her, inside her. A tight little coil of heat deep within her began to curl tighter still, then tighter, and tighter...and tighter...and tighter. And then, without warning, that coil burst free, blasting heat throughout her body. She cried out again at the eruption, convulsing against Connor. He held her firmly against him as she trembled in the aftermath, as the conflagration gradually quelled, as her body went limp against his. Little by little, her fingers loosened on his shirt, until she felt as if she would simply slide to the floor in a glorious puddle of completion.

But he caught her capably, wordlessly scooping her into his arms and carrying her into her room. She was helpless to stop him when he peeled her slip over her head and tossed it aside, pushed back the covers and laid her gently on the bed. But she felt strangely uninhibited as she lay naked before him. And she shamelessly drank in her fill of him as he stood beside the bed and undressed, his gaze darting over her body, from her face to her breasts to her hips to her legs, then retracing the visual journey all over again.

She let her own gaze wander, too, over every part of him that he revealed. Although she had known he was a big man, she'd had no idea how beautifully formed he was. His shoulders were broad and solid. And his torso was a landscape of rippling musculature covered by a rich scattering of dark hair that arrowed down into the waistband of his trousers. And then he was removing those trousers, too, and his briefs along with them, until he stood before her quite naked, his body gloriously silvered by the moonlight that splashed through the open French doors.

Even that part of him she knew a lady should never find fascinating, but from which she simply could not look away. He was quite aroused by now, she noted, quite... adamant, quite...inflexible, quite...

Oh, my.

"Why, Miss Winona," he said, his voice a velvet caress that parted the semidarkness and undulated over her nude body, "didn't anyone ever tell you it was impolite to stare?"

She smiled, but felt no obligation or desire to direct her attention elsewhere. "It isn't impolite to stare at a thing of beauty," she corrected him. "And you, Connor, are quite the magnificent specimen."

"Magnificent," he echoed with a chuckle. "Oooh, I like the sound of that."

"And I like..." But shyness overcame her sudden burst of boldness, and she found herself unable to finish whatever she had intended to say.

Connor, however, wasn't about to let her off the hook. "What do you like?" he asked when she declined to say. "Tell me, Winona. Tell me everything you want me to do to you."

She shook her head. "I can't."

"Why not?"

"I'm too...too..." But she couldn't even finish that statement. Being the kind of man he was, she was certain he would know exactly what to do.

He watched her carefully for a moment, then smiled. "All right," he finally said as he took a step forward, "then *I'll* tell *you* all the things I want to do to you."

"Oh, Connor, no," she whispered. "Don't do that. You'll embarrass me."

But he only continued to smile as he joined her on the bed. He lay on his side next to her, tangling his legs with hers, pulling her close, until not even the merest breath of air separated their bodies. His flesh was warm satin against her, shadowing her from shoulder to toe, and all she could think about was how much she wanted him. More of him. All of him.

"Will it embarrass you when I tell you I want to kiss you?" he asked softly.

She shook her head. "No."

"Will it embarrass you when I tell you that I want to kiss more than just your mouth?"

Heat seeped through her at his confession, but she shook her head again. "No."

"Will it embarrass you when I tell you that I want to fill my mouth with your breast?"

Now a burst of heat flashed in her belly, but she shook her head once more. "No. It won't."

"Will it embarrass you when I tell you that I want to fill my mouth with other parts of you, as well?"

His comment puzzled her. "Other parts?" she asked. "What other parts?"

Her confusion must have amused him, because Connor began to chuckle in earnest then, a dark, rich sound full of promise.

"You don't know what I'm talking about, do you?" he asked.

She shook her head, having no clue.

His smile grew broader. "You really don't have any idea?"

She shook her head again. "No. I'm sorry. I don't."

His grin now grew absolutely predatory. "Don't be sorry," he told her. "I'm sure as hell not."

"Connor…" she said, confused by what he was saying. Or, more specifically, by what he was *not* saying.

"Just wait," he told her. "You'll see."

And before she could ask him what he meant, he was kissing her again, rolling her backward onto the bed, until she felt the cool crush of the sheets on her heated back. As promised, he kissed her, deeply, masterfully, then he moved his mouth to graze her cheek, her jaw, her throat. Sighing,

Winona threaded her fingers through his soft hair, marveling at the silkiness. Connor dipped his head lower with every brush of his mouth over her skin, until she felt the flick of his tongue over the ripe peak of her breast.

And then he was indeed filling his mouth with her, sucking hard on her tender flesh. And then her heart was beating faster, and her breath was coming more raggedly, and her blood was racing through her veins at a dizzying speed. He held her breast firm in one hand as he tasted her again and again, each pull of his mouth more demanding than the one before. Winona tightened her fingers in his dark hair, holding his head in place as he nuzzled her, suckled her, consumed her. Then, suddenly, his mouth was gone, and he was moving his head lower, over her flat torso, tasting her navel as he passed it.

For a moment she wondered what he was doing. Then she felt his hands at the insides of her thighs, urging them open. He reached for a throw pillow that had been pushed to the foot of the bed and shoved it under her bottom, forcing her hips higher. When Winona finally glanced down to see what he was up to, she saw his dark head duck between her legs, and then—

Oh! Oh, *then!* Oh, good heavens! She felt the merest flick of his tongue against her, once, twice, three times, then a more thorough, more maddening taste. Again and again he stroked his tongue over her, even opened her with his fingers to sip at her more thirstily. And all Winona could do was gasp for breath and grip the edge of the headboard above her and hold on for dear life as he devoured her.

Just when she thought she would burst from the sensations spiraling through her, Connor pulled himself away and slowly moved his body back up alongside hers. By now, Winona could do little more than lie there, her body slick and slack from its response to his ministrations. But she heard him chuckle, felt him drop a kiss on her shoulder, and she smiled.

"I've never..." she whispered weakly. "No one's ever... I never realized..."

"Shh," Connor said softly against her ear. "We've only just begun, sweetheart. We have so many things to discover together."

She started to reach for him, but he brushed a brief kiss over her mouth and rose from the bed.

"Why...?" she asked.

"I need to take care of something before we go any further," he told her. Then he reached for his trousers and withdrew his wallet, digging in it until he located whatever he had been looking for. Winona watched with mixed feelings as he donned a condom before returning to her bed. But she said nothing, and neither did Connor, and perhaps that was for the best.

When he returned to her, he rolled her to her side away from him, then spooned his body close to hers. She was going to ask him why, then she felt the pressure of his shaft, so ripe and hard, pressing against her bottom, and she understood why. It was exciting this way. It was intoxicating. His hands drifted narcotically over her front as he kissed her shoulder and neck. Then he cupped one breast in sure fingers and slid his other hand down her torso, flattening it over her belly.

Instinctively, Winona lifted her leg and draped it over his thigh, and Connor took advantage of her movement, pressing himself more intimately against her. Before she realized his intention, he was entering her from behind, pushing her body back toward his to deepen his penetration.

Every bit of breath left Winona's lungs in a feverish rush at their joining. Never had she imagined herself capable of such an uninhibited response to a man. Never had she imagined herself making love this way to anyone. Yet with Connor, it all felt right and natural and good. So she nestled her bottom against his pelvis, reveling in the hiss of satisfaction he expelled when she did.

"Oh, yes," he murmured. "Oh, Winona. Oh, you feel so good."

A thrill of triumphant excitement shot through her when she realized she was having the same effect on him that he had on her. She felt powerful. She felt potent. She felt *alive*. Again and again she matched his rhythm, pushing herself backward with every thrust he made forward. And when he dipped his hand between her legs, burrowing his fingers in her damp flesh, she nearly cried out her need for more. His pace grew more rapid, and she reached back between their bodies, matching him, touch for touch. Then, just when she thought she would explode with wanting him, he withdrew from inside her.

She was about to voice her objection when he rolled to his back and pulled her astride him, thrusting up into her again. Winona bucked wildly, intuitively, against him as he filled his hands with her breasts and drove himself in and out of her. For long, wild moments, they coupled eagerly, until, with one final thrust, Connor went rigid beneath her. Winona's own release followed immediately on top of his, and she did cry out this time, because she simply could not keep her feelings inside any longer.

For one solitary, singular moment, they seemed transfixed in time and place. Then Connor's body went lax, and Winona crumpled over top of him. He rolled them both to their sides, facing each other, and pulled her closely, fiercely, to his heart. He buried his face in her hair and mumbled something fierce and incoherent into the tangled tresses. Winona wasn't sure, but she thought he told her he adored her.

And then, before she could stop herself, she mumbled against his chest, "Oh, Connor. I love you, too."

Connor never did fall asleep at Winona's house, even though she slipped into a blissful slumber at his side not long after their second coupling. Funny how panic and terror had a way of keeping a person awake.

He gazed down at the sleeping form beside him, noting the ease with which she cuddled against him, enjoying the warmth of her body pressed to his, marveling at the way he had bunched a handful of her silky hair in one fist, as if he needed to cling to her in whatever way he could.

And the only thought wheeling through his brain, over and over and over again, was, *What the hell have I done?*

Because as he gazed down at the woman who was sleeping so contentedly at his side, Connor realized something that shook him to his very core. He didn't want to let Winona go. Ever. And that, quite frankly, scared the hell out of him.

His first instinct was to bolt. To ease himself carefully out of her bed, get dressed as silently as he could and take off for parts unknown, never to return. He needed to think about this, needed to figure out what the hell he thought he was doing. How could he have made love to Winona when he had no business even talking to her? How could he have let her believe things about him that simply were not true? How could he have allowed her to think he was someone he wasn't? Hell, he hadn't even told her his real name.

Worse, by making love to her, after everything she'd just revealed to him, Connor had led her to believe he cared for her in ways he couldn't possibly care about any woman. He'd let Winona think he loved her. He'd let her believe that the two of them had a future together. A substantial future together. A permanent future together. Because he'd understood enough of what she'd told him about her broken engagement to know that she never would have made love with him tonight if she hadn't thought that was what he was offering her. Love. Commitment. Permanence.

Dammit.

He really was the biggest son of a bitch who ever walked the planet, Connor thought as his panic began to multiply.

He never should have allowed things to go as far as they had with Winona. She deserved a hell of a lot better than him. But he hadn't been able to help himself. He hadn't been able to resist her. When he'd seen her standing outside in the pale light of the rising moon, the wind nuzzling her hair around her face, her blue eyes filled with so much longing... When that ribbon of urgency and hunger had unwound so completely inside him, and he'd realized how badly he wanted her, how badly he *needed* her... When he'd understood that she cared for him the way she did...

Something inside him had just...snapped. He wasn't sure what or why. But in that moment, he had only known he had to make love to her. He *had* to. And damn the consequences, anyway. And now that he had made love to her...

Ah, hell. Now he didn't know what to do. He'd never responded to a woman the way he had responded to Winona. He'd never even come close. Making love to her tonight had been...

He couldn't even think of words to explain it. Indescribable, that's what making love to Winona had been. Her response to him had been incandescent, virtue mixed with desire, innocence mixed with eroticism. And an intuitive passion for which Connor had been completely unprepared. What Winona had lacked in knowledge, she had more than made up for in instinct and enthusiasm. Together, the two of them had generated an explosive reaction.

And that reaction scared him. Because he'd never felt anything like it before.

Damn. He would meet a woman like Winona right when he was living a big, fat lie. What was he supposed to tell her now? She thought he was someone else completely. Hell, she'd just made love with a man whose real last name she didn't even know. She'd all but told him before they made love that she loved him. And as if that hadn't been enough, she'd gone and spelled it out for him in the aftermath. She'd said it not once but twice. The first he might have been able to dismiss as careless words uttered in the heat of passion. But the second time...

The second time they had been cuddling and coherent, and she had looked him right in the eye and said, "I love you, Connor," before dipping her head to his chest and falling asleep.

And the thing of it was, he didn't *want* to dismiss her words. He was *happy* that she loved him. But God help him, he hadn't been able to say the words back to her. Because he just didn't know if he felt the words. He'd only been in love once before in his life. And it hadn't been anything like this. That time had been anxious and worrisome and gut-wrenching and even horrible at times. With Winona the things he felt were good. They were warm and tender and decent. He felt happy with Winona. So it couldn't be love, right? It had to be infatuation.

Hell, he honestly wasn't sure he was capable of feeling love anymore, not after what happened the first time. Not after his feelings had been trampled in the dirt the way they had. Certainly, he didn't see himself getting tied down to anyone anytime soon. Not even Winona. Even if she had done a damned good job of obliterating the image of nearly every other woman he'd ever known from Connor's mind. Even if he had absolutely no desire to see anyone else at the moment. Even if he couldn't really envision himself with anyone other than her for the rest of his life....

Run, he told himself again. *Beat it. Hie thee hence.* That was what he always did after he'd made love to a woman. He told her that what the two of them had just shared had been phenomenal, then he kissed her goodbye, and then he left. And those women never minded. They never expected him to hang around. A couple had flat-out shown him the door when they were finished, without so much as an "I'll call you."

But Connor had never minded. Sex had never been anything more to him than a way to let off steam and satisfy a few urges. A natural response to a natural instinct. And that was what it had always been to the women in his life, too.

Until now.

Now he'd gone and bedded a woman who had feelings for him. And for whom he had feelings himself. And he was shocked to realize that, with Winona, he didn't want to run. He didn't want to beat it. He didn't want to hie himself anywhere.

So instead, he only nestled his body closer to hers, pulling her nearer, tucking her head beneath his chin. He knew he wouldn't be sleeping tonight.

But he'd be damned if he would run.

Ten

As the fates—who were doubtless wetting themselves with laughter over Connor's predicament—would have it, the Bloomington cops got a very nice break in the Winona's prostitution case the following morning. A really good break, too, one that would enable them to close in on the restaurant perhaps as soon as the following day, once they got things organized.

But Connor had to leave the investigation to local boys that day—and that night. And in spite of all the hours he'd clocked on the investigation, he was perfectly happy to sacrifice the arrest. The last place he wanted to be when it went down was at Winona's, seeing her face as the cops rolled into her establishment like locusts, making arrests and closing her down until further notice. He wanted to be able to identify himself to her as a cop, and explain himself and his actions over the last few weeks, before she saw him wearing a blue windbreaker and wielding a Glock. Before she saw him busting people in her restaurant, and drew her own—erroneous—conclusions.

Especially since he still couldn't say exactly how erroneous her conclusions would be.

Because once Winona found out who and what Connor really was, she would conclude that he had been lying to her since the day they met. And, of course, she would be right. She would conclude that he was not the person she had thought him to be. And, of course, she would be right. She would conclude that many of the things he had said to her were grounded in total fantasy. And, of course, she would be right. She would conclude that he was a big, fat, lousy, son of a bitch heel. And, of course, she would be right.

She would conclude that he didn't care about her. And there, at least, she would be wrong. Dead wrong.

Because Connor did care about Winona. In ways he had never cared about anyone before. In ways he had never thought he *could* care about anyone. Those feelings had only multiplied after the night the two of them had spent together. Although he never had really slept the night before, he had dozed once or twice, and enjoyed some very nice dreams. And as the first rays of sunlight had spilled into Winona's bedroom through the still-open French doors, he had watched her awaken in his arms, bit by bit. And he had felt himself coming apart inside, bit by bit.

Because as he had watched her eyes flutter open and her lips part for her first conscious breath, as he had enjoyed the soft skim of her hair gliding silkily over his naked body, as he had felt the heat of her body suffusing his... Well. It had hit him in an almost blinding shock of awareness that he wanted to wake up in such a way every morning. Every morning for the rest of his life. And he hadn't known what to do.

So he had made love to Winona again, slowly, carefully, thoroughly. And then he had told her he needed to leave, to go to work, and she had nodded her understanding and smiled. She had asked if she would see him tonight. He had told her no, he had a previous engagement. Her smile had fallen some when he said it, as if she feared he might not be telling her the truth. Then she had told him that that was okay, she had an engagement herself that night, and wouldn't be home until late, anyway.

And something inside Connor had grown chilly then, when he realized just how many lies there were between them.

Ironically, though, Connor had been telling Winona the truth that morning. He *did* have a previous engagement tonight. A real engagement, too—the social kind. The kind you had to write on your calendar months in advance. The kind you only got allowed into with an engraved invitation. The kind that had fine food and wine. The kind where you had to wear a monkey suit. The kind where you had to watch every damn word that came out of your mouth to make sure you never said the wrong thing—because if you did, your great-aunt Pearl on your mother's side would whup you upside the head, but good.

The kind your great-aunt Pearl on your mother's side held once a year and expected *everybody* on your mother's side to attend *or else.*

Nobody said "No" to Auntie Pearl's invitations. Nobody. Which was how Connor now came to be wearing a damn monkey suit on his day off—his dark blue with a wine-colored tie, because it was his most conservative, and Auntie loved conservative. And it was how he came to be standing in a room filled with people, some of whom just so happened to be his four brothers and one sister and their assorted dates/fiancé(e)s/escorts/what have you. And it was how he came to be feeling restless and uncomfortable because he really wanted to be with Winona instead.

But he couldn't turn down Auntie's invitation—'cause *nobody* said no to Auntie Pearl. Or else. And he couldn't have brought Winona with him, either, even if she hadn't had a previous engagement herself, even though his engraved invitation had included the engraved words "and guest." Because if he had brought Winona as his guest, she would have found out that he wasn't really Connor Montgomery, Bloomington businessman, but was instead Connor Monahan, Marigold vice cop. And—call him an alarmist—that just might have caused her to start asking questions he still wasn't prepared to answer.

Oh, what a tangled web we weave, he couldn't help thinking. He would have finished the adage, but he wasn't sure how it went after that. He did know, though, that the last word was *deceive.* It was, after all a word with which he'd had more than a nodding acquaintance for quite some time now.

He sighed as he shoved the troubling thought aside and did his best to focus on the here and now. Ironically, both of his parents had been excused from Auntie Pearl's big bash, because even Auntie didn't expect them to get on a plane and fly up from Ocala for her annual Autumn Affaire. Well, Auntie *expected* them to, but she didn't get miffed when the elder Monahans weren't able to make it. Well, not *too* miffed, anyway. Not really. Just because she took it out on the rest of the Monahan clan by making them eat shrimp puffs and miniquiches and drink wine out of pansy little glasses, that didn't mean anything, right?

Right.

At any rate, now Connor found himself standing in the ornate ballroom of the expansive estate Auntie had called home since marrying his late uncle Holman nearly sixty-five years ago, at the tender age of sixteen. Auntie had been sixteen, at the time, not Uncle Holman. Uncle had been fifty-two. But that was another story. Now Auntie lived alone, save her personal trainer, Helmut, in the vast, Victorian mansion surrounded by towering oaks and maples, perched on a green, grassy hill in the middle of one hundred green, grassy acres of a green grassy farm, midway between Bloomington and Marigold...in the bog down in the valley-o.

A string quartet played in one corner of the ballroom, and scores of people mingled about, either dancing or drinking or snacking on canapés that looked as if they would make great ammunition when flung from the end of one of those little forks Connor had no idea what to do with. On one side of him stood his brother Rory, who was cooing softly to his fiancée things Connor was certain he didn't want to hear. On his other side, his sister Tess was murmuring something undoubtedly equally cloying to *her* fiancé. And Connor could think of nothing worse than being caught in the middle of so much mushy, gushy drivel. In a word, ick.

Man. The Monahans were dropping like flies. Tess had started it a few months ago by getting herself imaginarily knocked up with a nonexistent mob baby, something that had brought out the protective instincts in Will Darrow, who just so happened to be the best friend of Finn Monahan, the oldest Monahan brother. Then Will's protective instincts had turned into altogether different instincts, and Tess had just recently discovered that she was very truly pregnant with a very existent, nonmob baby—Will's baby, to be precise.

Fortunately, Will had done right by Tess. Not only had he had the decency to propose marriage to her, but he'd had the good sense to fall head over heels in love with her, too. Convenient, that, seeing as how the five Monahan brothers would have really hated to kick Will's ass after him being such a good friend for so many years. Now that wouldn't be necessary, because come November, he'd be making an honest woman out of Tess, and Tess would be making an honest man out of Will. And Connor was certain that the two of them would live happily ever after.

But then, no sooner had Tess and Will gotten things settled than Connor's older brother, Sean, had mixed himself up with Marigold's local "free spirit"—read "oddball"—Autumn Pulaski. Somehow Sean had lost a bet—or maybe he'd won it; Connor honestly couldn't remember now—and had ended up dating Autumn for longer than her proscribed lunar month—it was a long story. Now the two of them were planning to marry in December. And they, too, Connor was sure, would get completely mired down in all that happy-ending stuff.

And then the minute that had all begun to settle down, Connor's older brother, Rory—*Rory,* the epitome of the "absentminded professor" if ever there was one—had gone and fallen in love, too. Hell, Connor would have sworn Rory didn't even know *how* to fall in love. His brother's brain was so crammed full of historical dates and data, Connor wouldn't have thought there was room in there for him to even notice the existence of a beautiful woman, let alone end up proposing marriage to her. But in two months' time, Marigold, Indiana's, resident librarian, Miriam Thornbury, would become Mrs. Rory Monahan. Who would have ever tho—

Thornbury, Connor thought again as panic seized him. Oh, God. Rory's fiancée's last name was Thornbury, just like Winona's. At the very back of his brain, he'd probably had that knowledge for some time, but he honestly hadn't made the connection until now. He'd only met Rory's fiancée a couple of times, and he hadn't really paid attention to her last name, having enough trouble keeping women's first names straight in his head. Until now, he'd only thought about Rory's fiancée, Miriam, as either Rory's fiancée, Rory's fiancée, Miriam, or just plain Miriam. He hadn't thought of her in terms of Thornbury. But now that he did…

Oh, no. No, please…

"So, Miriam, can I ask you a personal question?" he

said suddenly, interrupting whatever maudlin little exchange she and Rory were still indulging in.

The cooing lovers halted their mushy stuff long enough to turn and gaze at Connor as one. Rory, dressed in a suit much like Connor's, peered at him through his horn-rimmed glasses, his black hair rumpled, his blue eyes only vaguely registering the fact that someone other than Miriam even existed in his universe. Miriam, dressed in a short, strapless, black velvet number with her dark-blond hair tumbling over her bare shoulders—and looking nothing like Connor figured a librarian should look—seemed equally perplexed by Connor's sudden appearance in her otherwise warm, fuzzy, Rory-oriented world.

"Hmm?" she asked vaguely. Then, with a brief shake of her head, she seemed to come around. "I mean…what question?"

Connor noted her blue eyes and the dark-blond hair again, the full mouth and high cheekbones, and boy, did he see a resemblance to Winona in that moment. Or maybe, hopefully, he was only imagining that, he thought. Maybe the two women didn't know each other from Adam. Or Eve. Whatever.

"Do you, ah…have any brothers or sisters?" he asked her.

Her expression would have been the same if Connor had just asked her to recite the Preamble to the American Constitution from memory. As did Rory's. Then again, Rory *could* recite the Preamble to the American Constitution from memory. But that was beside the point, and Connor pretended not to notice that his brother and his brother's intended were both looking at him as if he were nuts.

"Why do you ask?" she asked.

Connor feigned indifference, even managed to force a shrug that he was sure was sort of convincing. "Just curious."

"Well, I have a big sister," she said. "Her name is Winona. She lives not far from here, in fact. In Bloomington."

Oh, *dammit*.

"She owns a wonderful restaurant there," Miriam added.

Double dammit.

"One called, appropriately enough, Winona's," she finished with more than a touch of pride lacing her voice.

Dammit, dammit, dammit.

"Does she?" Connor asked, hoping nobody noticed that his entire reality was about to come crashing in on him. Hooboy. This was just what he needed. Until recently he had been looking to bust Rory's future sister-in-law for pandering and God only knew what other crimes. What were the odds on *that*?

Naturally Connor knew now that Winona was innocent of any crimes, which was mighty convenient, all things considered. But there was still that small matter of his current—and future—situation with Winona. No matter how things turned out with her—and truly, Connor still didn't know how things with Winona were going to turn out—he was going to have a tie to her for the rest of his life, in the form of her sister, his future sister-in-law.

Not to mention Connor's future sister-in-law was going to want to thump him, but good, no matter how things turned out, once she found out he'd initially been investigating her sister for pandering and peddling flesh and any number of other licentious crimes. Not to mention that, if Connor broke Winona's heart, his future-sister-in-law was going to want to thump him even better. Not to mention that Rory was going to be torn between the feelings of his new sister-in-law, Winona, or standing up for his blood relation, Connor.

Gee. Talk about being the family who put the *fun* in dys-*fun*ction...

"Funny you should ask about Winona tonight," Miriam piped up again. "Because your aunt Pearl hired her to cater this party. When she comes out from the kitchen again, I'll introduce you.''

Out from the kitchen? Connor thought frantically. *Again?* he thought even more frantically. Winona was here at his aunt's house? Now? He had simply lucked into missing her so far? He could stumble upon her at any minute?

Dammit, dammit, dammit, DAMMIT.

Without thinking, Connor grabbed his brother's arm and pulled him close, then steered him out of Miriam's earshot. ''Look, whatever you do,'' he whispered anxiously, ''do *not* introduce me to Miriam's sister, okay? And if Winona does see us together, you are *not* to introduce me as Connor Monahan, your brother.''

''What are you talking about?'' Rory asked, looking vaguely horrified by his brother's sudden attack of amnesia. ''Of course you're my brother. Of course you're a Monahan.''

''Not tonight, I'm not,'' Connor insisted. ''Not to the caterer. And somehow you've got to keep Miriam from mentioning me to her sister.''

Rory expelled a confused chuckle. ''What's Winona got to do with anything? Why are you acting this way?'' He reached for Connor's drink. ''I think you've had enough, little brother. I'm cutting you off.''

''Are you nuts?'' Connor asked, holding his drink close. ''I need this now more than ever.''

Rory eyed him with much confusion. ''You still haven't told me what Winona's got to do with anything.''

''She just can't know who I am, that's all.''

''Why not?'' Rory asked. ''She's not one of your criminals. She isn't…'' He halted abruptly, his expression changing drastically. ''Don't tell me you're investigating Winona for something.''

Connor said not one word, but only gazed at his brother solemnly.

Rory emitted another one of those strange, uncomfortable chuckles. "But she's…she's… Connor, she's as pure as the driven snow! She can't possibly be guilty of a crime."

"I know that," Connor said. "Don't you think I know that?" Before he could stop himself, and without considering the implication behind his words, he added, not a little frantically, "And even if I hadn't already known it, I sure as hell would have realized it after what happened last night."

Now Rory eyed him with much suspicion. "What happened last night?"

So much for being pure as the driven snow, Connor thought, biting back a wince. "I can't talk about it. Not now. Not yet."

"This is why you were in her restaurant last month, when Miriam and I were there, isn't it? Because you're investigating her. What on earth has she done?" Rory demanded. "No, wait a minute," he immediately backpedaled. "What is it you think she's done? Because I can tell you right now, Connor, the woman is harmless."

"I can't discuss it," Connor said. "I know she hasn't done anything. But right now, she can't know…"

"What?" Rory asked.

"She can't know her restaurant is under investigation."

"*What?* Under investigation for what?"

"I can't talk about it, Rory. Not yet. Just don't let her know who I am." He darted his gaze quickly around the room. "In fact, I have to get out of here. This place is crawling with Monahans. And if she finds out who I really am…"

"Auntie will never forgive you if you leave before dinner," Rory said.

"I know."

"If she gets hold of you, she'll whup you upside the head. But good."

"It's a chance I'll have to take."

"But—"

"Rory, I have to go. Give my best to Auntie, and tell her something came up. Something work related. She loves that cop stuff I do. She'll understand. Tell her it was a triple murder. She'll like that."

"You work vice," Rory reminded him.

"Then tell her it's the biggest heroin bust the state of Indiana has ever seen, and that I'll probably have to draw my weapon, and maybe even fire off a shot or two. It won't go over as well as a triple murder, but it'll have to do."

"But, Connor—"

"I have to go," he said again, cutting his brother off.

And then he made good on his assurance by bolting from the room without a backward glance. He didn't stop moving until he was seated at the wheel of his car, and realized belatedly that he was still gripping the cut crystal tumbler that held his Scotch and water. Hastily, he dumped the drink out the window and set the glass on the passenger seat. Then he ground the key in the ignition and threw the car into gear.

It was only when he hit the city limits of Marigold twenty minutes later that Connor remembered something very important. He remembered that Cullen was still at Auntie's party. Cullen Monahan. His brother. His *twin* brother. His mirror image. And Winona was going to see him there.

Once again without thinking, Connor slammed on the brakes and spun the steering wheel, wreaking a U-turn the likes of which the Indiana State Police would never see again. God willing, they wouldn't see it now, either. He had no idea what he was going to do. But one thought circled around and around in his head, like a great white shark honing in on a fat, naked swimmer. He had to get back to his aunt's house. Now. Because there was one thing Auntie hated more than not having her blood relations show up at her house for a party.

Auntie hated it when all hell broke loose in her home.

* * *

Winona was collecting the last of the canapés from Mrs. Greenup's buffet in the ballroom when she glanced up and saw Connor standing on the other side of the room, chatting with a small group of people. She smiled. Not just because she was delighted to see him, but because she realized then that he hadn't been lying to her, after all, that morning, when he'd told her he had a previous engagement.

He must know Pearl Greenup in some capacity, she thought, and Mrs. Greenup had invited him to her annual soirée, and Connor hadn't been able to turn her down, even if he might have preferred being with Winona tonight. She herself had seen what a formidable force Mrs. Greenup could be. Winona certainly wouldn't have been able to turn down an invitation from the woman. She got the impression that nobody said no to Pearl Greenup. Or else. So she couldn't fault Connor for telling her he needed to be here tonight instead of with her.

She was more than a little relieved to discover that he had told her the truth. Even after the night the two of them had spent together, Winona had been overcome this morning by the inexplicable feeling that he was hiding something from her. She had no idea why she should feel that way, or what he might *be* hiding, but she hadn't been able to shake the feeling, no matter how hard she'd tried.

So she was glad to know now that Connor had told her the truth. Her smile grew even broader as she watched him throw back his head and laugh at something one of the other people had said. He had the most wonderful laugh, she thought. Until now, she'd never heard it so robustly.

Then she saw him loop his arm around the waist of the woman at his side, and her smile fell. And then she saw him dip his head to brush a quick kiss over the woman's mouth and murmur something low that made her smile. And then Winona felt herself withering inside.

No, he hadn't lied about having a previous engagement, she thought again. But there were, evidently, a few other things he had kept to himself. She was beginning to understand now, what he had been hiding from her. She only hoped that the woman with him was a girlfriend and not a wife. Then again, what difference did it make? she thought. What mattered was that he had lied to her. Horribly.

Before she realized what she was doing, Winona found herself striding across the room toward him. She skimmed her hands nervously down over the skirt of her sapphire-blue, Victorian-era gown, then reached up to tuck a few errant strands of hair back into the bun she had fastened at the top of her head. She wondered why she was bothering with her appearance, then realized it was because the woman with Connor was so...so...

Honestly. The woman's attire fairly screamed, "Come and get it!" A brief miniskirt—and was that *leather* it was made of?—and an even briefer vest—with no shirt beneath—and high heels that were more heel than shoe. Her hair was an ebony cascade of silk that rolled down to her hips, and long jet earrings dangled nearly to her shoulders. And all Winona could do was wonder what, if this was the kind of girl he normally dated, Connor could ever have wanted with a nice, old-fashioned girl like her in the first place.

Winona was amazed at how numb and cold she felt inside as she approached the group of people. Somehow, she managed to keep her steps even and unhurried as she drew nearer, and she stopped when there was still a nice polite distance between her and Connor. And in a perfect display of well-bred courtesy, she did *not* wrap her fingers around his throat and squeeze the life out of him when she had the chance—and every right—to do so.

"Why, Mr. Montgomery," she said by way of a greeting. "What a surprise to find you here. I didn't know you knew Mrs. Greenup."

Connor turned at the sound of her voice, but he eyed her with some confusion. If Winona hadn't known better, she would have sworn he had no idea who she was. And in an odd way, he did seem different to her somehow, too. He'd gotten a haircut, she could see, but that was the only real difference she could discern. Nevertheless, he did seem a stranger in many ways.

"I'm sorry," he said, "but I think you must have mistaken me for someone else. My name isn't Montgomery."

She forced a laugh, but something inside her grew a little chilly, because his expression changed not one whit. Surely, he wasn't going to deny that he was who he was, she thought. Surely he wasn't going to deny that he knew her. Especially not after what the two of them had shared the night before. Perhaps this was some kind of morning-after— or, in this case, *evening*-after—game that lovers played with each other, Winona told herself, a game she would naturally know nothing about. She'd only played the game twice, after all. And she'd been terrible at it the first time.

Of course, viewing the evidence currently placed before her eyes, there was every indication to suggest that she hadn't been particularly good at it the second time, either. Because Connor had run right out to find himself a new playmate, hadn't he?

"Oh, stop," she said, hoping she was injecting the right amount of playfulness in her voice even though she was feeling anything but playful at the moment. "You know perfectly well who I am, and perfectly well who you are, too. *Mr. Montgomery,*" she added meaningfully.

But Connor still looked confused. "Well, I'll concede that I do know who *I* am," he said. "But my name is *Monahan,* not Montgomery. I'm Cullen Monahan, to be specific." And he said it with utter conviction and without a trace of humor. So much so, that Winona began to worry.

She couldn't understand it. Either Connor was flat-out

lying to her, or else he'd received a severe blow to the head that had left him utterly disoriented, or else he had an absolute twin wandering around out there in the world.

"Oh," she said, hoping she masked her own confusion. "I…I apologize. You look exactly like someone else. A man of my acquaintance named Connor Montgomery."

Now the man's expression did finally change. He smiled quite happily, looking more like Connor than ever. "I should have realized," he said. "You mean Connor *Monahan,* of course. He's what you might call my evil twin."

"I…I beg your pardon?" Winona stammered.

Now the man laughed. "Sorry. Old joke. No, really, I do have a twin brother named Connor. I'm sure that's who you've mistaken me for. Connor Monahan. Not Connor Montgomery."

Winona shook her head. "No, I'm certain his last name is Montgomery. I know him quite well. And he is most certainly your twin."

The man shook his head, now looking more bewildered than Winona felt. "That's odd," he said. "I've never known Connor to misrepresent himself. You're sure he said his name was Montgomery?"

"Quite sure."

"How strange…" His voice trailed off for a moment, then the man who identified himself as Cullen Monahan lifted his flattened palm to his forehead, and his expression cleared. "Of course. You met him in an official capacity. That would explain it."

"Official capacity?" Winona echoed. "What do you mean?"

"He's a cop," the other man said. "A vice detective for the Marigold, Indiana, Police Department. You must have met him when he was working on a case. He sometimes uses an assumed name for such things."

"A case?" Winona echoed. "A policeman? Marigold?

No, no, no. That's not possible," she insisted. "The man I know is a business executive. He works in Bloomington."

Cullen Monahan shrugged. "Then he's not my twin brother."

"But he is your twin," she said weakly.

Cullen Monahan gazed at her with much interest then, as if he thought her a bit…touched. Or perhaps, she couldn't help thinking, his expression was more in keeping with a man who was worried that he had said much too much about something he shouldn't have mentioned at all.

Oh, no, she thought as a heavy weight settled in her mid-section. *Connor, please. Please, no…*

What on earth was going on? she wondered. This man said he had a twin brother named Connor. Winona had met a man named Connor who looked *exactly* like this man. They must be one and the same. But why would Connor have given her a false name for his last name? Why would he have told her he was a businessman, when he was, in fact a police detective?

Then Winona remembered something very important. She remembered that Connor Montgomery had never told her specifically what he did for a living. She had simply assumed he was a businessman, and he had never offered her any indication to the contrary, had never suggested to her that he was anything else. He'd never really told her *what* he did for a living, not in so many words. Yet he'd never contradicted her assumption, either.

But why the false name? she wondered further. Why would he lie to her about something like that? Unless…

You must have met him when he was working on a case.

But what kind of case would he be working on that involved Winona? That made no sense. She was the most upstanding, law-abiding citizen around. Might it have something to do with the restaurant? But her business was as upstanding and as law-abiding as she. Why, she never even cheated on her taxes. Never. What on earth could he have to investigate at Winona's? And why hadn't he simply identified himself as a police detective up-front, and asked her any questions he might have? It was almost as if he—

As if he were investigating *her*.

Something hot and unpleasant fired in her belly. That must be it, she thought. For some reason—who on earth knew why?—she was the subject of a police investigation. And Connor Montgomery—no, Connor *Monahan*—was the one who was doing the investigating.

Oh, no, she thought again as that heavy weight descended to the pit of her soul. *Connor, please. Please no...*

That was why he had initially come into the restaurant, she told herself. That was why he had watched her so intently for so long. That was why he had asked her out in the first place. It all made sense now. She'd wondered from the start why he would bother with a woman like her, when he was so clearly suited to another type of woman entirely. And she'd never been able to understand why he kept coming back, when they obviously had nothing in common. And last night...

Oh, heavens, last night. Last night couldn't have meant anything to him. Certainly not what it had meant to her. Last night, he'd simply seen an opportunity—an opportunity she had offered most freely—and had taken advantage of it. What man wouldn't?

Here she'd been thinking last night had been as special to him as it had been to her. Here she'd been thinking that the reason he had made love to her was the same as the reason she had made love to him. Because he loved her. Because he envisioned a future with her. But clearly, he hadn't understood anything of what she'd told him about her broken engagement. He hadn't understood the implications of her avowals. He hadn't realized she had fallen in love him. Not until she had *told* him, she thought. And even then, even after he knew how she felt about him, he'd made love to her again. He'd used her. Then he'd left her.

No wonder he'd had a previous engagement tonight.

Last night she would have done anything for Connor. Last night she *had* done anything for him. She'd given herself over to him completely, in ways she hadn't even known she could give. Because she had loved him. Because she had thought he loved her, too. Because she had been thinking— hoping—that the two of them had a future together. A future that would last forever. She had thought he cared for her. But clearly, he had simply thought what she was offering— and oh, my, how shamelessly she had offered it—was just too good to pass up.

Foolish, foolish Winona, she chastised herself now. When was she going to learn? When would she stop being such a…such a…such a *cow?* Such an easy-virtued, give-it-away- for-free cow?

Men only wanted one thing from women, she reminded herself ruthlessly. And when they got that one thing, they lost all interest in anything more. She never should have given herself to Connor the way she had. She never should have trusted him. She never should have let things go as far as they had.

One thing was certain, she thought. She would never give of herself that way again. Not when it hurt so much to lose it.

Eleven

Winona was so caught up in her sorrow and confusion that she barely heard the soft scrape of sound that heralded the arrival of someone else in the Greenup kitchen right after the guests had seated themselves for dinner. Thinking it was someone who was taking exception to the lack of a saltshaker because they had no idea what to do with a salt-cellar, or some such thing, she was surprised to glance up and find Connor standing on the other side of the deserted kitchen, staring at her. Or was it Cullen? she wondered. What had the other man been wearing? She couldn't remember now.

This man—whoever he was—clearly did not have sartorial splendor in mind, however. Because his suit, although it had probably been impeccable when he had donned it, was now in a state of disarray that could only have come about because he had given up all hope of…something. Winona couldn't possibly have known what. Nor, she discovered, did she much care. All she knew was that this man—whoever he was—had lied to her. Because she saw then that it was indeed Connor, and not Cullen, who had entered the kitchen. She knew that, because he gazed at her with much familiarity. And because her body came alive the moment she beheld him.

"Hi," he said a little nervously.

"Hello," she replied coolly, clasping her hands together before her. Whether that was to keep her from wrapping them around his throat to choke the life out of him or to keep herself from reaching for him and clinging to him for dear life she wasn't sure. Either way, though, her reaction would have been troubling. So she only stood stock-still, returning his stare, and waited to see what he would say for himself.

He expelled a long, weary sigh. "Gee, judging by your reception, I guess it's true," he said.

"What's true?" she asked, even more coolly than before, clasping her fingers tighter.

Connor took a step toward her, and even though a wide kitchen island stood between them, Winona instinctively took a step in retreat. Her response made him halt in his tracks, but his gaze never left hers as he hesitated, shoving his hands deep into his trouser pockets. His mouth went flat, and his eyes darkened angrily. Somehow, though, she knew the anger was directed at himself and not at her.

"Word has it that you met my evil twin, Cullen, a little while ago," he began. "And that he volunteered some information about me that he had no business volunteering."

Winona notched her chin up defiantly. "No, you should have been the one who volunteered it," she said. "And you should have done so long before now. Long before—"

"Last night," he finished for her.

"Yes."

He nodded almost imperceptibly, then forced a smile that was in no way happy. "Leave it to an evil twin to mess things up,'' he said. But neither of them seemed to find much humor in the statement.

"That's interesting," Winona told him, "because Cullen said that you're the one who's evil.''

With his hands still buried deep in his pockets, Connor shrugged halfheartedly. "Yeah, well...tonight I guess I'm kind of inclined to agree with him.''

She missed not a beat in rejoining, "So am I.''

He studied her long and hard in silence for a moment, as if he were trying to impress her image upon his brain somehow. Then, very, very quietly, he told her, "Winona, I can explain.''

"Oh, I don't doubt that at all," she replied, every bit as quietly. "I don't doubt that you'll explain it very well.''

He seemed hopeful, eager, for a moment. "Then you'll give me a chance?''

"Of course," she said. "And once you've explained, then we'll part ways and never speak of this unfortunate incident again. In fact, we'll never see each other again. That will make it infinitely easier to keep from talking about it.''

His face went pale and slack at her declaration. "That's not...''

He blew out another exasperated breath, then he took another step forward, removing a hand from his pocket, lifting it as if he intended to reach out to her. Winona stepped back in retreat again, but the kitchen counter hindered her progress, and she bumped against it with her fanny. Connor took advantage of the predicament to hasten around the kitchen island and position himself in front of her. Before she had the chance to bolt, he dropped a hand on each side of her, gripping the kitchen counter hard, and effectively penning her in.

His heat and scent seemed to envelope her, and she was immediately carried back to last night, when their naked bodies had been pressed so intimately together in an entirely different fashion. She squeezed her eyes shut tight in an effort to chase the image away, but it only grew more graphic, more real. When she opened her eyes again, her vision was filled with Connor, and, mesmerized, she found that she simply could not look away. His face was only inches from hers, and she fancied she could almost see the dark turmoil swirling in his eyes. His lips parted fractionally, and it was all she could do not to push herself up on tiptoe and cover his mouth with hers.

Heaven help her, even now, even knowing what she did about him, she still wanted him. Still needed him. Still loved him.

Her heart was beating frantically in her chest, and her breathing had become heavy and erratic the moment he had penned her in. But he was no less affected than she, she saw. His own breathing was coming out in rapid, ragged rasps, and she could see his pulse beating nimbly at the base of his strong throat.

"We need to talk," he said intently, his eyes never leaving hers. "I mean, we *really* need to talk, Winona."

"Then talk," she said shallowly.

A burst of raucous, feminine laughter—Mrs. Greenup's, if Winona wasn't mistaken—bled through the kitchen door from the other side, reminding them that they were by no means alone.

"Not here," Connor told her. "And not now. When will you be finished?"

I'm already finished, she wanted to say. "I imagine I'll have everything here packed up by ten-thirty, and then I'll go home."

"I'll meet you there."

She shook her head. "No."

He looked panic-stricken at that. "But we need to talk. Come to my hotel, then."

She expelled an incredulous little sound and said, "Oh, I don't *think* so."

"It wouldn't be like that," he told her.

"No, you're right," she agreed. "It wouldn't be. I *won't* be. Ever again."

He said nothing for a moment, only continued to study her in that silent, desperate way. "You told me you'd give me a chance to explain," he reminded her.

So she had, Winona thought. "All right then," she said. "I'll meet you at my house at eleven. But don't think for a moment that there will be anything more than talking going on."

He met her gaze levelly, and her heart kicked up that funny rhythm again. "Do you think maybe there could be a little listening going on, too?" he asked softly.

"It depends on what you have to say," she told him evenly.

He nodded again, slowly, but didn't push himself away from the counter, or from Winona. Before she realized his intention, he dipped his head to hers and brushed his lips lightly over her own. The gesture almost undid her, so tender, so solicitous was it. And then he pulled himself away from her, taking a few steps backward, but never removing his gaze from hers.

"I'll meet you at your place at eleven," he said again.

Winona could only nod, because she had no idea what else to say. That seemed to be enough for him, though, because with one final, longing look at her face, her eyes, her mouth, he spun on his heel and departed the kitchen.

As he left, Winona couldn't help enjoying a good, long look at his back. Not because it was so beautifully formed and solid and sure. And not because she was remembering how it had felt the night before to curl her fingers so zealously into the hot, naked flesh that covered it.

But because she couldn't help thinking that she would be seeing it again very soon.

Connor didn't wait until eleven to drive to Winona's house. He went there immediately after leaving her in the kitchen at his aunt's house, without even explaining to his aunt Pearl where or why he was going. So Auntie would whup him upside the head the next time she saw him. But good. At this point, whuppings from great-aunts were the least of his worries. Especially when he turned the corner onto Winona's street and saw the tumble of blue and red lights illuminating her restaurant.

Oh, God, he thought. The cops were already here. They were raiding the place. That was supposed to be tomorrow. How could they have pulled everything together so quickly? How could they be doing this tonight? How could they be here when he and Winona still had so much to do and say?

He pulled his car to a halt behind one of the marked police cars, then flashed his badge as he exited the vehicle. A uniform waved him into the fray, and Connor ducked under the yellow police tape to gauge the climate.

Not good, he realized immediately. Worse than a circus. Already they had busted four people—two women and two men—and had all of them seated in the back of several patrol cars. Another woman was being led out the front door in handcuffs as Connor approached. Inside the restaurant things were even more chaotic. Uniforms and plainclothes alike were swarming, talking to some of the patrons and employees, arresting a couple of others.

Looked like one of Winona's hosts, a guy named Bart, was right in the thick of it. He was the one who'd organized the hookers, the one who was orchestrating their activities. He and his girls had been plying their trades right under Winona's nose for God only knew how long. And tonight it was all coming down on their heads.

Hoo-boy, Connor thought. They could be here all night. Winona was going to be crushed by the time this was through.

He stepped back outside, to see if he could find the principal detective on the case and offer his help. Then, as if thinking about Winona had conjured her appearance, he saw a car, one he didn't recognize, roll to a halt near where he had parked his own. The driver, he saw immediately, was his brother Rory. Rory's fiancée Miriam was in the passenger seat. And then the back door opened and Winona jumped out. Someone from the restaurant must have telephoned her at his aunt's house, to tell her what was going on. Now she stood in the street, gazing at her restaurant with so much anguish and terror the place might as well have been going up in flames.

Then again, Connor thought, in a lot of ways, it was. It was going to take some doing for Winona to recover from this. And not just the prostitution bust, either. But a whole host of other messes. Naturally, he couldn't help but feel responsible for the bulk of them.

His instincts commanded him to go to her, to talk to her, to comfort her. But his damnable reason stepped in to halt him. She was with her sister and future brother-in-law, he reminded himself, and she'd probably rather have them than him to take on the role of comforter right now. Connor had other obligations, anyway. Later the two of them could talk, he told himself. Later, he hoped, he could comfort her. But right now, he had a job to do.

Hours later, when the moon hung high in the sky, and the restaurant had finally emptied of everyone except Connor and Winona, the two of them sat in her dining room upstairs, each with a neglected cup of tea sitting on the table in front of them. Neither had said a word after the last official had left. They had only turned to look at each other through their exhaustion and disorientation, and had come to the silent and mutual agreement that they should go upstairs.

Connor had followed her up automatically, had watched without speaking as she mechanically made tea and poured it for both of them. Neither, however, had shown any interest in drinking it. Both of them had far too many other things on their minds.

Now Connor leaned back in his chair and stared at Winona, who was perched on the edge of her own seat with her body turned away from his, so that she was gazing off in the other direction. He told himself to say something, anything that might alleviate some of the tension that was burning up the air between them. But for the life of him, he had no idea how to begin.

Fortunately, Winona seemed not to have that problem, because eventually she murmured, "I can't believe a ring of prostitutes was operating out of my restaurant, right under my nose, and I never even knew it. And I can't believe one of my employees was the one running it."

Connor couldn't imagine what she must be feeling at the moment. To be betrayed once was pretty horrible. To have it happen twice, in a matter of hours, no less, must be devastating. Of course, Connor was still of the opinion that he hadn't betrayed Winona. Nevertheless he wouldn't blame her for taking exception to his exception.

But she wasn't the only one who'd been overwhelmed tonight, he thought further. The last few hours had been pretty devastating for him, too. He'd learned a lot about himself in the last few hours. And some of it still had him reeling.

"If it's any consolation," he said halfheartedly, "Bart and the girls said they chose your place because of the high-class clientele."

She emitted a single, humorless chuckle. "Yes, well, thanks to Bart and the girls, my clientele will now be highly nonexistent."

"Don't be so sure," Connor told her. "Your clientele may very well double now, because of the curiosity seekers."

"Wonderful. Now I'll have an entirely new reputation. My slogan won't be 'At Winona's, everybody feels at home' anymore. Instead, it will be 'At Winona's, everybody gets felt up.'" She propped her elbows on the table and buried her head in her hands. "How could I have let this happen?"

Connor rose from his chair and moved to the other side of the table, seating himself beside her. He wanted to reach out to her, to touch her, but he was afraid that she would rebuff him. So for long moments he only sat with his hands doubled into fists in his lap, watching her grow more and more withdrawn. Then, unable to tolerate even the small physical distance between them, he lifted one and splayed it open gently over her back.

Amazingly, she didn't recoil. She only continued to sit silently with her head in her hands, as if she'd given up hope on everything.

"Winona, you couldn't have known," Connor told her. "You're too nice a girl to have ever suspected something like that was going on. It's no wonder they operated right under your nose without you realizing. In your world, things like prostitution and illegal behavior don't exist. In your world, there's nothing bad, only good."

"That may have been true once," she said without moving. "But not anymore."

He hesitated only a moment before replying, "Yeah, well, it sucks the first time it happens, but you learn to live with it."

She did move then, lifting her head slowly from her hands and turning to gaze at him fully. "What do you mean?" she asked.

He met her gaze levelly for a moment, not sure what to tell her, not sure if she would believe him, not sure if it would make a difference, anyway. Then he decided, hell, he had nothing to lose. Nothing but Winona. And he feared she was already halfway gone to him.

So, quietly, he began, "You're not the only person in the world who's ever been betrayed, Winona."

She said nothing in response to his comment, only continued to gaze at him in silence. But he had her attention, he could tell that much. So, reluctantly, he continued.

"Not long after I graduated from college, I met a woman. To make a long story short, she knocked me off my feet." He smiled sadly. "I'd never met anyone like her. She was..." He sighed. "She was just really special, that's all."

Winona arrowed her brows down as she listened to him, and Connor got the impression that her reaction now was similar to the one he'd had as he'd listened to her talking about her beloved Stanley the day before. Good, he thought. If she cared that much, then maybe they still had a chance to work things out.

"I fell in love with her, Winona. Totally, hopelessly in love with her," he said, heat seeping through his belly when he saw the stricken look that crossed her face. Oh, yeah. She cared. She cared a lot. "At least, I thought I loved her," he corrected himself quickly. "At the time I didn't think it could be anything but love. She had me tied in knots, never knowing if I was coming or going. I just... I was crazy about her."

"So what happened?" Winona asked, her voice low and rough. "Did you...did you ask her to marry you?"

Connor shook his head. "There were times when I thought about it," he said honestly. "But I could never bring myself to pop the question. Something held me back. Then, about nine months after we started dating, there was one night when she told me she couldn't see me because she had to work, and then that night, I saw her out in a restaurant with another man."

Winona's gaze never veered from his, and he wished like hell he knew what she was thinking. "She was two-timing you?"

"You could say that," Connor told her. "Turns out the man she was with that night was...her husband."

"Her husband?" Winona echoed incredulously.

He nodded. "She'd been married for years, and I never knew. Here I had made her the center of my life, and she had another life entirely that I knew nothing about. And as if that weren't enough, when I confronted her, she told me that all I was to her, all I had ever been to her, was a means to an end. Her husband had been unfaithful to her, and she wanted to hurt him the same way. His affair had lasted ten months, and that was how long she had planned to stay with me. After ten months she would have left me, because she would have used me for everything she needed, and she would have told her husband all about us. But I screwed that up for her when, by sheer dumb luck, I stumbled on her and her husband out that night."

Winona still said nothing, still only gazed at him in silence. Still only looked stricken and sad and confused.

"She got what she wanted, though," Connor continued. "The night I saw her with her husband, she introduced me to him as her lover. Told him all about what we had done and why she had done it. The guy then proceeded to escort me outside, where he then beat the hell out of me while she looked on. All that time I thought she had loved me the way I loved her. But I'd never meant anything to her. Nothing. She'd only been with me to hurt her husband."

Very quietly Winona said, "And instead, you were the one who got hurt."

He nodded.

"I know how you feel."

"Maybe," he said.

She studied him in silence for a moment longer. Then, very softly, she asked, "Why did you first come into my restaurant?"

Connor had already promised himself he would tell the total and complete truth about everything. He'd lied to her too many times, for too long, to be anything but honest now. So, in response to her question, he told her, "The local police received an anonymous tip that a ring of call girls was operating out of your restaurant, and when they looked into the matter, they found out that it was true. They just didn't know who was heading the operation up, and they didn't know how the ring was being run.

"I was working an investigation in my hometown of Marigold that overlapped the one here, and I ended up working with the Bloomington team. The local boys sent me in as a decoy, hoping one of the women would approach me and we could tie the matter up neatly. That was why I couldn't tell you who I was, Winona. Because I was investigating the place."

"Just the place?" she asked.

"No," he said. "I was investigating you, too."

She swallowed with some difficulty before asking him, "You thought I was a prostitute?"

He shook his head, and he could see a small flicker of relief ease her expression. Until he told her, "I thought you were the madam."

Her expression closed up again at his declaration, and her eyes filled with tears. Please, not that, Connor thought. He could stand almost anything, but he couldn't tolerate the realization that he'd made Winona cry again.

"And I guess after last night," she said, "you think of me as little more than a who—"

"Winona," he interrupted her. "After last night…" He sighed heavily. "I'm not sure what I think. Just that… You're not what I thought you were."

"And you're not what I thought you were, either."

"I'm *everything* you thought I was," he countered immediately. "I gave you a phony name, Winona. Not a phony person."

"I don't see the distinction."

"I couldn't tell you my name, because it would have jeopardized the investigation. But everything else I've showed you of me over the last couple of weeks… That was all real. It was all true. Everything you know about

Connor Montgomery is true of Connor Monahan. We are one and the same person. And anything that happened between you and me, *every*thing that happened between us, that was all real and true, too.''

She jumped up from her chair then, doubling her fists at her sides. "I know it was real," she said. "That's the problem. It doesn't matter who you are. I fell in love with you, anyway. And I'm going to be in love with you forever.''

"And I fell in love with you, too!" Connor shot back without thinking. "I'll be in love with you forever, too!"

He might as well have just told her he was a pod person from another planet, so profound was Connor's surprise at hearing what he'd just blurted out.

Winona, too, seemed stunned, because her mouth dropped open, her eyes went wide, and she whispered hoarsely, "You what?"

Connor bit back the panic that welled up at the back of his throat, and he told himself he shouldn't be so damned surprised. He did love Winona. He knew that now, with all his heart and soul. He just hadn't recognized the feeling before now because it was one he'd never felt in the past. Even years ago, when he'd thought he was in love, love hadn't been what he felt at all. What he'd felt years ago for the woman who had betrayed him had been something else entirely. It had been passionate and emotional and intense, to be sure. But it had also been desperate and anxious and insecure.

That, he realized now, had been infatuation. This thing with Winona... This was something else. It was warm and loyal and boundless. It was constant and definite and certain. It was endless. And it went soul deep.

It was love. What else could it be?

"I love you," he said again, less frantically this time. He stood, too, cupping his hands on her shoulders. "I love you, Winona, and I don't want to live my life without you.''

The tears in her eyes tumbled freely as she said, "I don't know if I can believe you. You've told me so many lies."

"I never lied to you," he countered.

"Didn't you?"

"No," he stated unequivocally. "Maybe I let you believe some things I probably shouldn't have let you believe, but I never lied to you."

"You told me your name was Montgomery."

"I had no choice."

"But it was a lie."

"All right!" he conceded. "That was a lie. But nothing else was. None of it. Oh, Winona, don't you see?" he pleaded. "I never lied to you about the important things. I never lied to you about this."

And with that, he looped an arm around her and pulled her close, covering her mouth with his. For a moment she struggled against him, fisted her hands loosely on his chest and tried to push him away. Connor told himself he would stop if she made him, that he would never, ever force her to do anything she didn't want to do. But he knew she wanted him. He knew it. He could tell by the way she had looked at him. He could tell by the way she had told him she loved him.

And he wanted her, too. He loved her, too.

The realization of that hit him square in the brain again, as if Aunt Pearl herself had just whupped him upside the head, but good. He loved Winona Thornbury. And he would never be the same again.

Her hands on his chest loosened then, the fists gradually uncurling until her fingers turned the other way and twisted in the fabric of his shirt. Connor deepened the kiss as she pushed her body closer to his, then moved his hand between them to close it over her breast. She sighed against his mouth when he touched her, then urged one of her own hands lower, down toward his taut abdomen. For long moments they only explored each other, kissing and caressing, until he thought he would come apart at the seams.

Those damnable buttons, Connor thought as he brushed his fingertips over the front of her dress. He was really going to have to talk to her about her wardrobe. Because he wasn't going to do battle with every dress she owned, every time he wanted to make love to her. After they got married, he'd just have to explain to her that—

He jerked his mouth from hers the moment the idea formed in his brain. Marriage. To Winona. Of course. Why hadn't he thought of that before?

"Marry me," he said suddenly, impulsively. Somehow, though, the statement didn't feel impulsive at all.

She stared at him as if he'd gone mad. "What?" she asked.

"Marry me," he repeated. "Please. Promise me you'll spend the rest of your life with me."

"But, Connor," she said, her voice laced with nervousness, "we have so many things to settle, so many things we need to—"

"We can even have a long engagement and settle things over it. But promise me, Winona, that you'll stay with me forever." He smiled. "Because I can't make love to you unless I know you're committed."

She smiled back. "I should probably be committed for this but... Yes. I promise I'll stay with you."

"Forever?"

"Forever."

"You'll marry me?"

"I'll marry you."

"When?"

She laughed. "I don't know, Connor. Can't we talk about that later?" She moved her hands to the buttons of his shirt and began to unfasten them one by one. "Right now I need you. I want you. I love you. Tell me again that you love me, too."

"I love you, too," he stated with all certainty. "And I want you. And I need you. Right now."

He closed his eyes for a moment, just to make sure he wasn't imagining things, just to be certain he hadn't been dreaming all this time. It shouldn't be this easy, he thought. It shouldn't be this simple.

Then again, they were in love, he reminded himself. What could be simpler than that?

Winona undid the last of his buttons and pushed her hands beneath the fabric of his shirt, shoving it from his shoulders. Connor released her long enough to let the garment slide over his arms to the floor. Then, without even thinking now about what he was doing, he lifted her by the waist and set her on the table, and moved himself immediately between her legs. She smiled wickedly as she curled her fingers over his bare shoulders, then bucked her hips forward as he drew nearer. Grinning mischievously back at her, he began to slowly push the skirt of her dress higher, over her knees, her thighs, her hips.

"These," he said as he moved a hand to the waistband of her panties and yanked hard, "have got to go."

Winona smiled as she leaned back on her elbows, and lifted her bottom from the table so that he could pull them off. Connor did so with rapt efficiency, tossing them to the floor near his shirt. Then he loosed the button on his trousers, tugged down the zipper and freed himself completely. He sprang out hard and fully aroused, and Winona continued to lie back on her elbows, opening herself to him completely. He took a step forward, lifted her legs and braced them over his shoulders, then positioned himself to bury himself thoroughly inside her.

They both cried out at the depth of his penetration, but he simply could not wait any longer to possess her and be possessed by her. Later they could make love again, and they could take their time and do all the things to each other that they wanted to do. Now though...

Hungrily, desperately, he thrust into her, again and again and again, the friction of their motion creating a delicious heat that seeped through both their bodies. Connor wanted to make it last, but there was too much welling up inside him for him to keep it all in. And in a near-blinding rush of heat and sensation, with a cry of both triumph and defeat, he spilled himself inside her.

For one long moment neither of them moved, both seeming too dazed by what they had just done to speak. Then Winona reached for Connor, and he met her halfway, linking his fingers with hers.

"Never lie to me again," she told him.

"I'll be as honest with you as I've always been," he replied.

"Take me to bed, Connor," she said with a smile.

And smiling back at her, he readily complied.

Epilogue

Spring was in full bloom the day of Winona and Connor's May wedding, and she was glad they had decided months ago to say their vows in her garden. Mother Nature had cooperated beautifully, and now the lilac bushes were brimming with fat purple blooms, lavender stretched from one shrub after another along the side of the house, and lily of the valley spilled abundantly along the line of the fence. Best of all, plump, heavy peonies of white and pink and violet dribbled petals along the walkway bisecting it all, as if acting the role of flower girl for the bridal party.

Of course, if she and Connor had simply waited a few years to get married, their brand-new niece Rosemary, whom Connor's sister Tess cradled close to her breast, could have played the part of flower girl. As it was, however, one month old, they had all decided, was just a tad early for such a role. And besides, there was no way she and Connor could wait years to get married. It had been hard enough waiting for months.

Still, they were delighted that the first member of the next generation of Monahans could be here for this occasion. Especially since Winona knew that the next member wouldn't be far behind. Her sister had sworn her to secrecy for now, but Miriam hadn't been able to wait to tell her a few weeks ago that she and Rory were expecting, too, with a due date in December. Winona wouldn't be surprised if Sean and Autumn shared similar news soon.

She turned her attention to Connor's twin brother, Cullen, and wondered when he and his new wife would make such an announcement. Who knew? Maybe she and Connor would even beat them to it. Not that Winona was in any hurry to become a mother, but there was that biological clock situation to think about. Certainly Connor made her feel ten years younger, in spite of the decade that separated them. Still, they had talked about having children soon.

First, of course, they would have to marry. She was, after all, a nice, old-fashioned girl. She wouldn't dream of having a child out of wedlock. As it was, she and Connor had been lucky she hadn't gotten pregnant that day in September when they'd made up so beautifully. It went without saying, though, that she'd moved past that pesky premarital sex hang-up she'd had for some time. Oh, my goodness, had she moved past that. Many, *many* times over the past several months. But they'd been very careful about taking precautions against pregnancy since that single time they'd gone without. Even if they hadn't been cautious about much else, sexually speaking.

Indeed Connor had proved to be a very adventurous lover, and Winona had been thrilled to learn all the tricks of the trade. So to speak. Surprisingly, though, she'd been able to teach him a thing or two, as well. About anticipation. About taking a leisurely approach. About making it last a long, long time.

Goodness, it was warm for May, she thought suddenly.

They should probably start the ceremony before someone succumbed to heat prostration. Or something.

The ceremony was to be a small one. Only immediate family had been invited, and she and Connor would have only one attendant each—Miriam would be her matron of honor, and Cullen, Connor's twin, was to be his best man. But a few of Winona's neighbors had halted on the sidewalk beyond the gate to greet the happy couple and murmur good wishes. And a few of her employees had stopped by to drop off some gifts. The restaurant was closed today, of course, but would be reopening tomorrow. Winona's business was so good these days, she didn't want to interrupt the flow. Even a few of Connor's friends from the Bloomington PD had stopped by to wish them luck. Winona wasn't going to chase any of the well-wishers away. She wanted as many people as possible to join her on this, the happiest day of her life.

Oh, no, wait a minute, she thought as she saw Connor approaching. This wasn't the happiest day. Not quite. The happiest had been the day she'd walked out of her kitchen and seen Connor seated in her restaurant for the very first time. She'd known nothing about him then, except that he'd made her feel something she'd never felt before. Over the last eight months, she'd learned more about him than she had ever imagined she would. But none of it—none of it— mattered more than how she felt about him.

They strode up the garden path together, arm in arm, toward the minister, who stood framed by the trellis upon which morning glories blossomed. Miriam smiled at her from one side of the trellis, her vintage lavender gown offsetting her blue eyes and dark-blond hair beautifully. Cullen, Connor's mirror image, stood on the other side in a pale-gray suit. Connor himself wore a dark-navy-blue suit, which enhanced the color of his eyes with breathtaking clarity. She only hoped her white Victorian gown edged with lace and seed pearls and buttons could hold a candle to him.

But judging by the appreciation that lit his eyes, she succeeded quite well in that candle-lighting business. In fact, judging by the way Connor was looking at her now, she'd guess that much more than a candle was burning. She hoped they didn't have to linger long at the reception inside. She couldn't wait to leave for their honeymoon.

"Are you ready?" he murmured as they drew nearer the priest. And she knew he was talking about too many things to list.

She nodded. "As they say in the vulgar contemporary vernacular, bring it on."

He grinned at her. "Oh, baby. Do I have plans for you."

They covered the final few steps together, clasping hands and gazing into each other's eyes, never once noticing anything else. Winona spoke her vows to Connor with utter conviction, and as he spoke them back to her, she was overwhelmed by how honest and honorable and decent he was and how he would love her forever and ever.

And as he slipped a perfect circle of gold over the ring finger of her left hand, Winona reveled in the knowledge that, in this day and age, she had somehow managed to find herself such a nice, old-fashioned boy.

*   *   *   *   *

January 2002
THE REDEMPTION OF JEFFERSON CADE
#1411 by BJ James

Don't miss the fifth book in BJ James' exciting miniseries featuring irresistible heroes from Belle Terre, South Carolina.

February 2002
THE PLAYBOY SHEIKH
#1417 by Alexandra Sellers

Alexandra Sellers continues her sensual miniseries about powerful sheikhs and the women they're destined to love.

March 2002
BILLIONAIRE BACHELORS: STONE
#1423 by Anne Marie Winston

Bestselling author Anne Marie Winston's Billionaire Bachelors prove they're not immune to the power of love.

MAN OF THE MONTH

Some men are made for lovin'—and you're sure to love these three upcoming men of the month!

Available at your favorite retail outlet.

Where love comes alive™

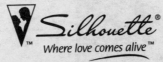

If you enjoyed what you just read,
then we've got an offer you can't resist!

Take 2 bestselling love stories FREE!

Plus get a FREE surprise gift!

Clip this page and mail it to Silhouette Reader Service™

IN U.S.A.
3010 Walden Ave.
P.O. Box 1867
Buffalo, N.Y. 14240-1867

IN CANADA
P.O. Box 609
Fort Erie, Ontario
L2A 5X3

YES! Please send me 2 free Silhouette Desire® novels and my free surprise gift. After receiving them, if I don't wish to receive anymore, I can return the shipping statement marked cancel. If I don't cancel, I will receive 6 brand-new novels every month, before they're available in stores! In the U.S.A., bill me at the bargain price of $3.34 plus 25¢ shipping and handling per book and applicable sales tax, if any*. In Canada, bill me at the bargain price of $3.74 plus 25¢ shipping and handling per book and applicable taxes**. That's the complete price and a savings of at least 10% off the cover prices—what a great deal! I understand that accepting the 2 free books and gift places me under no obligation ever to buy any books. I can always return a shipment and cancel at any time. Even if I never buy another book from Silhouette, the 2 free books and gift are mine to keep forever.

225 SEN DFNS
326 SEN DFNT

Name	(PLEASE PRINT)	
Address	Apt.#	
City	State/Prov.	Zip/Postal Code

* Terms and prices subject to change without notice. Sales tax applicable in N.Y.
** Canadian residents will be charged applicable provincial taxes and GST.
  All orders subject to approval. Offer limited to one per household and not valid to current Silhouette Desire® subscribers.
  ® are registered trademarks of Harlequin Enterprises Limited.

DES01   ©1998 Harlequin Enterprises Limited

Coming in January 2002 from Silhouette Books...

THE GREAT MONTANA COWBOY AUCTION
by
ANNE McALLISTER

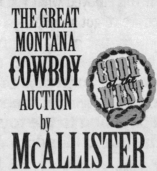

With a neighbor's ranch at stake, Montana-cowboy-turned-Hollywood-heartthrob Sloan Gallagher agreed to take part in the Great Montana Cowboy Auction organized by Polly McMaster. Then, in order to avoid going home with an overly enthusiastic fan, he provided the money so that Polly could buy him and take him home for a weekend of playing house. But Polly had other ideas....

Also in the Code of the West

Available at your favorite retail outlet.

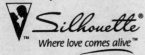
Where love comes alive™

Visit Silhouette at www.eHarlequin.com

PSGMCA

DYNASTIES: THE CONNELLYS

A brand-new Desire® miniseries about the Connellys of Chicago, a wealthy, powerful American family tied by blood to the royal family of the island kingdom of Altaria

Filled with scandal, mystery and romance, *Dynasties: The Connellys* will keep you enthralled in 12 wonderful new stories by your favorite authors, including Leanne Banks, Kathie DeNosky, Caroline Cross, Maureen Child, Kate Little, Metsy Hingle, Kathryn Jensen, Kristi Gold, Cindy Gerard, Katherine Garbera, Eileen Wilks and Sheri WhiteFeather.

Don't miss this exciting program, beginning in January 2002 with:

TALL, DARK & ROYAL
by Leanne Banks
(SD #1412)

Available at your favorite retail outlet.

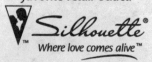
Where love comes alive™